"Why did you come back, Brody?"

"Forgot something."

"What? Your lucky penny?" Mallory asked sarcastically.

"Nope."

She caught her lower lip between her teeth. He watched her steadily, the hint of a smile hovering at the corners of his mouth. "Then what?"

Brody sauntered over, never lifting his gaze from hers. "This." He framed her face with his hands, and she felt herself flushing as his touch sparked a response. He slowly bent forward, his gaze still locked on hers, and she vibrated with anticipation.

He's going to kiss me, she thought, surprised by her own lack of panic. *And this time I'm not scared. I'm not scared of Brody at all. I want him to kiss me. I want to kiss him back.*

WHAT ARE *LOVESWEPT* ROMANCES?

They are stories of true romance and touching emotion. We believe those two very important ingredients are constants in our highly sensual and very believable stories in the LOVE-SWEPT line. Our goal is to give you, the reader, stories of consistently high quality that may sometimes make you laugh, sometimes make you cry, but are always fresh and creative and contain many delightful surprises within their pages.

Most romance fans read an enormous number of books. Those they truly love, they keep. Others may be traded with friends and soon forgotten. We hope that each LOVESWEPT romance will be a treasure—a "keeper." We will always try to publish

LOVE STORIES YOU'LL NEVER FORGET
BY AUTHORS YOU'LL ALWAYS REMEMBER

The Editors

MAN SHY

CATHERINE MULVANY

BANTAM BOOKS
NEW YORK · TORONTO · LONDON · SYDNEY · AUCKLAND

MAN SHY

A Bantam Book / March 1998

ISBN 0-553-44604-5

Published simultaneously in the United States and Canada

Bantam Books are published by Bantam Books, a division of Bantam Dou-
bleday Dell Publishing Group, Inc. Its trademark, consisting of the words
"Bantam Books" and the portrayal of a rooster, is Registered in U.S.
Patent and Trademark Office and in other countries. Marca Registrada.
Bantam Books, 1540 Broadway, New York, New York 10036.

PRINTED IN THE UNITED STATES OF AMERICA

OPM   10 9 8 7 6 5 4 3 2 1

For Lynette Cooley,
my number one fan

ONE

"This is pathetic," Mallory Scott muttered, *this* being the fact that she was huddled in a corner of the Blue Russian, waiting for Mr. Right. She knew Brunswick, Oregon's one and only gay bar wasn't the traditional hunting ground for a straight single female, but she was desperate. Dial-A-Date Escort Service hadn't panned out. Nor had any of her lonely-hearts ads.

And this isn't gonna either. Hoping to drown her niggling doubts, she gulped the last of her screwdriver, grimacing at the taste.

Kyle Brewster laughed at her expression. "I told you to order a Coke."

"Liquid courage." Mallory's smile was grim but determined. With just over a week left before her sister Lindsey's wedding, the search for a hunk-of-the-century escort had assumed a frantic urgency. This meeting Kyle had arranged with his old fraternity brother was her last hope. Her only hope. A feeble hope that was fading fast.

Mallory glanced at her watch. The man was already

ten minutes late. She slumped forward in defeat, resting her forehead on the table. "He's not coming."

"Relax." Kyle gave her shoulder a reassuring pat. "Punctuality has never been Brody's strong suit."

Slowly she sat up, staring myopically at Kyle over the tops of the glasses that had slipped to the end of her nose. "And patience has never been mine." She signaled for a refill.

"He'll be here. Don't worry." Kyle nudged her wire frames back up to the bridge of her nose. "Maybe you ought to go easy on the booze, though. You're not used to it."

"I need all the help I can get," she objected, then sighed heavily. "Correction. What I need is a man. And not just any man, either. A real dream babe. Somebody so completely studly he'll wipe that smug, pitying expression off Lindsey's face forever."

Kyle sipped his Chablis. "Don't worry. Brody Hunter's twice as sexy as any leading man in Hollywood."

The bartender set a fresh drink in front of her. "Who's twice as sexy as any leading man in Hollywood, and when are you going to introduce me?" He winked at Kyle.

"Sorry, Tim. This one's spoken for."

"*C'est la vie.*" The bartender shrugged. Gathering up Mallory's empty glass and crumpled napkin, he returned to the bar.

"You'd better be right about your friend." Mallory forced herself to swallow a dose of orange-flavored medicinal vodka. "This is not a situation where just any warm body will do. I need a major hunk."

"Drumroll, please. Here comes the hunk of your dreams now." Kyle nodded toward the entrance.

Looking up, Mallory choked on her drink. Kyle considered the man in the doorway a hunk? Hunk of what? Road apple cobbler?

"You're kidding." With filthy, tattered clothes, heavy-duty black stubble, and long, tangled hair, Kyle's hunk was about as appealing as the winos who hung out at the bus depot on North Oregon Street. "He's a bum."

"Undercover cop," Kyle corrected her. He waved the rough-looking thug over to their table.

Mallory held her breath. The man smelled even worse than he looked, and he looked downright terrible. Up close she could see the grime staining his knuckles, the grease matting his uncombed hair. Had he been working undercover or underground? Struggling to maintain a calm demeanor, she shot her friend a quick, nervous glance. This was a joke, right?

Kyle stood up, doing his impression of the genial host. "Mallory, this is Brody Hunter, my old fraternity brother. Brody, say hello to Mallory Scott."

Brody Hunter looked like a former fraternity man about as much as Kyle looked like Arnold Schwarzenegger, which was to say, not at all.

He shoved his fists in the pockets of his grubby black raincoat. "I'd shake hands, but I took an unplanned detour through the sewer earlier this afternoon. Caught the little creep who's been mugging senior citizens in the park, though." The gravelly voice died abruptly.

His gaze caught and held Mallory's, sending a shiver rippling down her spine. Okay, so maybe her first impression was wrong. Maybe there was a little hunk potential buried under all that grime and wild hair. Brody's eyes were a pale, silvery gray, startling in such a swarthy face. He had a good, strong nose, well-marked brows, and a very nice mouth. Though maybe nice was the wrong word. Sexy was closer. Drop-dead gorgeous closer yet. Mallory drew a shaky breath. *He's gay*, she reminded herself.

"Have a seat." Kyle indicated the chair between his and Mallory's. "The other customers are getting nervous."

Not just the other customers. Mallory hid her trembling hands in her lap.

The corners of Brody's mouth twitched. "Yeah. They're probably trying to decide whether I'm gonna flash 'em or blow the place to kingdom come. Sorry about the clothes. Things went down in a hurry, but the paperwork took forever. I didn't have time to change. Hope I'm not ruining your reputation."

"Other than the somewhat pungent aroma, you're fine. Mallory's the one who has the clientele agog. They don't get many females in here."

As Brody settled onto the chair its rattan frame groaned in protest. He was a big man, as tall as Kyle, but heavier—broad-shouldered, athletic. A wicked half smile twisted one corner of his mouth. "If anyone asks you later, just tell 'em she was a guy in drag."

Mallory stiffened. "I don't think that's funny."

Obviously her companions disagreed. Both men fought to keep their faces composed.

"It's not like I'm the only female in here, you know. Not ten minutes ago I saw a blonde slip into the manager's office. And unless I'm blind, there are two more *ladies* at the bar." Floozies, she'd almost said. There ought to be a law against baring that much cleavage.

Kyle and Brody exchanged a look.

"What?" she demanded. It took her a second, but she finally got it. "You mean they're men?"

"Transvestites," Brody said. "Listen, do they serve anything edible in this joint? I'm starving."

Kyle shook his head. "No food. Just drinks."

Brody groaned. "Why'd you set the meeting up here, then? Why not Chico's? I could really go for one of their chicken chimichangas."

"Truthfully, I was more concerned with anonymity than menu choice. I figured none of the Blue Russian crowd would be invited to Lindsey Scott's wedding. Whereas if we'd met at Chico's . . ."

Mallory nodded in agreement. As Brunswick's unofficial yuppie watering hole, Chico's was no place to maintain a low profile.

"Here." Kyle shoved the bowl of pretzels across the table. "Chow down on those."

Brody examined his filthy hands dubiously. "Maybe I'd better wash up first."

An excellent plan, in Mallory's opinion. His fingernails alone looked like they were good for anthrax, typhoid, dysentery, and six varieties of the common cold.

"It's a dirty job," Brody said, catching her gaze, "but somebody's got to do it." Grinning broadly, he headed for the rest room.

Maybe Brody Hunter wasn't soap-opera-star handsome like Evan, her ex-boyfriend and soon-to-be brother-in-law, and maybe his sense of humor was a little warped, but he did have a great smile. And he moved well too. Like a dancer. Or an athlete.

She sipped her drink and tried to picture the reaction if she showed up at the rehearsal dinner with Brody in tow. Their arrival would undoubtedly trigger her mother's temper. April Scott made no secret of her hatred of long hair on men. But it might be worth all the flak just to see the look on Lindsey's face. And Evan's.

Gradually Mallory became aware that Kyle was staring at her, his expression expectant.

"What?"

"Well, was I right or was I right? Didn't I tell you Brody was perfect?"

Mallory raised an eyebrow. "Define perfect."

"Open your eyes, kiddo. Under that veneer of grime lurks a genuine hunk. Admit it, he's a giant step up from your recent lonely-hearts disaster, Bobby Ray Hicks."

"And a Paul Bunyan cut above Ramon, the octopus from Dial-A-Date." She smiled. "You're right. And besides, this late in the game, I'm in no position to be picky."

"Then here's to last chances." Kyle clinked his glass with hers.

"Last chances," Mallory repeated, not sure she liked the sound of that. She took another sip of her screwdriver, shuddering at the taste.

"Cold?" Brody asked as he slipped back into the chair next to hers.

"No, I . . ." Glancing up, Mallory caught her breath in surprise. Soap and water had performed miracles.

"Do I pass?" A crooked smile lit his face.

She blinked, then smiled back. She knew it must be a pretty sappy-looking smile from the startled expression on Kyle's narrow, intelligent face, but at the moment she was too excited to care whether or not she looked like a brain donor. Good-bye, Mr. Hyde. Hello, Dr. Jekyll.

Lindsey, eat your double-crossing, man-stealing heart out.

Kyle cleared his throat. "Let's get down to business."

"Sure," Brody agreed. "Lay it all out." He tapped Mallory on the shoulder. "Pass me the peanuts, would you?"

"Peanuts?" she echoed, trying to ignore the tingling sensation that lingered in the wake of his casual touch.

Kyle gave her a strange look. "Yeah, you know. Little salty edibles. Look sort of like brown jelly beans."

"Oh, right. Peanuts." She shoved the bowl toward Brody, and he tossed a handful in his mouth.

Kyle drummed his fingertips on the table, obviously anxious to get this show on the road. "The thing is, Mallory needs a date for her sister's wedding."

Brody chewed thoughtfully, studying Mallory.

She squirmed around in her chair, feeling like a slide under a microscope.

Brody swallowed, then shook his head slowly from side to side. "Maybe I'm being dense, but I don't get it. Why would a woman like you need to be fixed up?"

Mallory felt her cheeks grow warm. "I—" Words failed her. Insults she was prepared for. Teasing she could deal with. But compliments threw her every time.

"What's the matter with the men in this town?" Brody demanded. "Are they blind?" He finished off the peanuts and started on the pretzels.

Mallory and Kyle exchanged a look. It's all yours, kiddo, he seemed to say.

She took a deep breath. "You just moved here, right?"

Brody nodded. "Couple months ago."

"Well, when you've been here a little longer you'll

realize that although our corner of eastern Oregon has its pluses—lots of sunshine, wide-open spaces, and recreational opportunities up the wazoo—eligible males are thin on the ground. I've been on the prowl for months now, ever since Lindsey and Evan announced their engagement—"

"Evan used to be Mallory's significant other," Kyle interrupted. "They dated for almost ten years."

"Eleven, but who's counting?" Stupid question. She was. Mallory drained her glass. "Ever since we were juniors in high school."

"What happened?" Brody sounded as if he were sincerely interested, not just being polite. Or maybe it was the cop in him, automatically switching to interrogation mode.

"Like Kyle, Evan's in broadcasting. When he was offered the newsteam anchor position at a Portland station, he jumped at the opportunity. Bigger market, more money. I planned to move to the Portland area to be near him as soon as my current contract was up."

"Mallory's a teacher. Fifth grade." Kyle rolled his eyes. "Talk about a glutton for punishment."

"So where does the sister come into it?" Brody asked.

Mallory narrowed her gaze. "Lindsey lives in Beaverton, a Portland suburb. She's a buyer for Nordstrom's and a real snake in employee-discounted designer clothing."

"I think you mean wolf, not snake. You're mixing metaphors. No more screwdrivers for you, my girl."

"Don't lecture, Kyle. I can tell when I've had enough. My ears tingle."

"Really?" Brody tugged gently at her left earlobe.

Mallory jumped like she'd been hit by an electric cattle prod. The sensation went way past tingle. More like tingle to the tenth power.

The curl of Kyle's lip said, I told you so.

Obviously, vodka packed more punch than the wine coolers she was used to. Lots more. She shuddered involuntarily. Why else would callused fingers lightly pinching her earlobe trigger shock waves that rocked her from head to toe?

Kyle shot her an enigmatic look. Still gloating, no doubt.

She stuck her tongue out.

He grinned.

"Go on, Mallory," Brody urged. "You were telling me about your sister."

"Right. Lindsey." Mallory frowned. "The conniving brat."

"Don't listen to her. That's just her injured pride speaking. Lindsey's all right. Boring, but basically decent."

"And gorgeous. Don't forget gorgeous." She sighed. "Kyle's right. I shouldn't blame Lindsey. It was mostly my fault. After all, I was the one who insisted that Evan look her up once he got settled. How was I to know he'd fall madly in love at first sight? I mean, he's known her since she was a scabby-kneed twelve-year-old. Who'd have thought makeup and an upscale wardrobe would turn a man's brain to Jell-O?"

"Your little sister stole your boyfriend," Brody translated.

"Bingo." Kyle gave him two thumbs up.

"And to add insult to injury, she asked me to be her maid of honor." Mallory took a deep breath. "Consequently, I need an escort for the festivities. Got plans for next Saturday?"

Brody blinked. "The day after tomorrow?"

"No, a week from this Saturday."

"What's wrong with Kyle?"

"I've already got a date," Kyle said. "Besides, everyone knows Mallory and I are just friends. We wouldn't fool anyone."

"Fool anyone?"

Mallory shifted in her chair, suddenly uncomfortable. "Well, you see, when my sister called to say she'd just become engaged to my boyfriend, all hell broke loose. Overnight I became an object of pity. Poor Mallory. Poor rejected, over-the-hill Mallory." She made a face. "I didn't mean to tell any lies. It just sort of happened."

"Lies?"

"Whoppers," Kyle said.

"Like?"

"Like Evan's defection wasn't the blow everyone assumed since I'd been secretly seeing someone else—a real drop-dead-gorgeous hunk of a male."

"And that's my role? I'm the drop-dead-gorgeous hunk?" Brody laughed in genuine amusement. "I take it Mel Gibson and Kevin Costner were all booked up."

"Actually," said Kyle, "you're more the Antonio Banderas type."

Mallory ignored his interruption. "Anyway, that's why I need you, Brody . . . to prove I'm not the pathetic loser everyone believes I am." Though come to think of it, propositioning a stranger in a gay bar was pretty damned pathetic.

Brody shook his head. "I don't know. . . ."

"What's to know? All you have to do is stand around looking sexy and mysterious. You don't even have to talk if you don't want to. I can tell everyone you're foreign, that you only speak Norwegian. Nobody around here speaks Norwegian."

"He doesn't look Norwegian," Kyle objected. "Too dark."

Mallory suppressed an impatient sigh. "Okay, so he can be Romanian. Nobody speaks Romanian, either."

Brody frowned. "Including me. Look, language aside, I'm still not sure I could pull it off."

Mallory studied his face. What was he trying to say? "Oh," she said. "Because of your orientation, you mean?"

"My orientation?" Brody arched an eyebrow.

She flushed. "Look, it doesn't matter to me. Live and let live, I always say. Heck, Kyle's one of my best friends, and any friend of Kyle's is a friend of mine."

Kyle smirked. "She means she doesn't mind that you're gay."

Brody's pale eyes bored into hers. "That's very broad-minded of you."

Mallory bit her lip. "I'm sorry if I said anything to give offense. The thing is, I'm desperate. Heck, I've tried everything from escort services to personal ads. All the applicants were a wash. Either they were weenie little weasels who wouldn't fool Lindsey for a second or they were way too eager to 'ring my chimes.' That's a direct quote, by the way, from Mr. Dial-A-Date. His name was Ramon and he looked like a gigolo. I swear to God the man had glue-on chest hair."

"So," said Kyle, "are you game?"

"Glue-on chest hair?" Brody's expression defied description, falling somewhere between incredulity and revulsion.

"And gold chains like somebody caught in a seventies time warp. I'm pretty sure he used mascara on his mustache too."

Brody blinked. "Mascara?"

"And nail polish."

"On his mustache?"

"No, of course not. His fingernails."

"What color?"

"Clear," she admitted, "but even so . . ."

Brody nodded in sympathy. "Even so."

Kyle smacked the table with his palm. "These digressions are all very fascinating, people, but to get back to the point, what do you say, Brody? Will you do it?"

"Do what, exactly? You're just talking about a date, right? A onetime shot? No strings?"

"More like a two-time shot, actually, counting the rehearsal dinner. But absolutely no strings," Mallory promised. She waited nervously for his answer. He was going to say no. She could feel it in her bones.

Brody shrugged. "Sure. Okay."

"Why does she think I'm gay? You been lying to the lady?" Brody stuffed a chunk of chicken chimichanga in his mouth. Kyle, taking pity on his famished state, had agreed to this dinner at Chico's. Unfortunately, he'd insisted that Brody shower and change first, which meant his poor stomach was only now, at a quarter to eight, getting relief.

"I wouldn't call it lying exactly." Kyle wiped his salsa-covered fingertips on a napkin. "When I offered to fix her up, she assumed that since you're my friend, you must be gay too. And then, when I arranged for her to meet you at the Blue Russian . . ." He shrugged.

Brody chewed slowly, thinking about it. "Sounds to me like you wanted her to jump to the wrong conclusion."

"Yes, well . . ." Another shrug.

"Well, what?"

"Mallory's a terrific person." Kyle paused, nodding thoughtfully and sipping his margarita.

Brody drained his second bottle of beer. "But?"

Kyle poked his enchilada, not meeting Brody's gaze. "But shy," he said. "A little repressed."

Brody nodded. That fit. Feature for feature, Mallory was one of the most beautiful women he'd ever seen, though she'd seemed determined to disguise the fact with glasses and baggy clothes. That prim little French braid of hers had driven him crazy. He'd kept wondering how she would look with all that pale hair loose on her shoulders, her *bare* shoulders.

And those eyes. Behind her glasses, Mallory Scott had the clearest, bluest eyes he'd ever seen, haunting eyes that seemed to see right down inside him. A little repressed? Maybe. But he'd be willing to bet there was heat beneath that cool exterior.

Kyle frowned. "Mallory clams up completely around most males, though she's never been that way with me."

"Let me guess. You don't threaten her because you're gay." He nodded. "And you figured if she knew I was heterosexual—"

"She'd freeze up. That icicle act of hers is the real reason she hasn't been able to find a date for the party. Anytime a guy shows a little interest—"

"She turns into a snow princess," Brody guessed.

"Right. And since I know how important this date is to her, I didn't want to give her an opportunity to shoot herself in the foot again."

"I see." So the woman had unplumbed depths. Great. "Look, if Mallory has problems . . ."

"None that need trouble you," said Kyle. "All she wants is an escort, not a lifetime commitment."

Which should have been a relief, since marriage did not figure prominently in his future plans.. His parents had done the wedding thing. Repeatedly. To date, he had four stepmothers, six stepfathers, and enough stepsiblings to populate a small continent. None of his parents' marriages lasted, which probably had something to do with the fact that infidelity was an honored Hunter family tradition.

He frowned at the glob of guacamole on Kyle's partially eaten enchiladas. "Good. 'Cause I'm definitely not looking for a wife."

"I'm not looking for a husband," Mallory told Brody. She waved a spoon to emphasize her point. "I'm perfectly happy being single. But my family just doesn't get it."

After leaving Chico's, Brody had shown up on Mallory's doorstep, armed with a list of questions and a couple of hot-fudge sundaes. In his experience, there wasn't a woman in a thousand who could resist the allure of chocolate.

He set his empty sundae dish on the trunk Mallory was using as a coffee table and settled back against the cushions of the love seat. "Families tend to tune out anything they don't want to hear," he said, thinking of his sister, Jenna, whose seemingly irrational behavior should have clued the family in that something was wrong. Unfortunately, no one had paid attention until it was too late.

Though they didn't look alike, Mallory reminded him of Jenna. She had the same quiet dignity, the same guileless gaze, the same air of vulnerability. "Families just don't listen," he said.

"Oh, they listen when it suits them." Next to him, Mallory scraped the last of the fudge from the bottom of her dish. Dressed in jeans and a T-shirt, with her hair straggling free of its braid to curl in tendrils around her face and a tiny smudge of chocolate on her chin, she could have passed for one of her own students. "Believe me, when they meet you, my family will be all ears, straining to hear every last detail about our imaginary relationship."

"So fill me in." He leaned closer to wipe off the chocolate with a corner of his napkin, but paused with his hand just inches from her face, arrested by the sudden look of panic in her eyes. "You missed a spot," he said, handing her the napkin. "On your chin."

Shifting her gaze away from him, she scrubbed at her chin. He watched in fascination as the color rose in her cheeks. What had she thought he was going to do? Kiss her? Not that the idea hadn't crossed his mind. But why such a strong reaction? She acted like she'd never been kissed before, yet surely, if she'd dated the same man for eleven years, she was accustomed to kisses. Kyle had warned him Mallory was shy, but her behavior was more than just a natural reserve. She seemed almost frightened.

Brody frowned. *Forget it, Hunter,* he told himself. *This woman's hang-ups are none of your damn business.* "So," he said, his voice carefully casual, "how exactly did we meet? No, let me guess. I was the tour guide on your trip to Romania, right?"

His words earned a smile. She met his gaze. "No, I didn't figure out the Romanian connection until this evening. Basically, all I told my family was that you were tall, dark, and handsome."

"What?" He widened his eyes. "No background? No occupation?"

"Not really. Though I did drop a few hints about covert operations." She winced in preparation for his reaction.

"I'm supposed to be CIA?"

She chuckled. "Actually, I pictured you more as a soldier-of-fortune type. Have bazooka, will travel."

Brody grinned at the image of himself in Rambo getup. "Does that mean I get to wear a headband and camouflage paint to the wedding?"

She shuddered. "Not unless you want everyone in town to think you're GI Joe."

GI Joe was what the newspaper had dubbed the rapist who'd attacked several Brunswick-area women in the last two months. The only lead the police had to his identity was that he dressed like a combat soldier. Of all his current cases, it was the one Brody was most anxious to solve.

"I guess that wouldn't be such a great idea." He turned to face Mallory more directly. "Do I have a name?"

Once again color flushed her cheeks and she refused

to meet his gaze. "I was thinking of it more like a nick-name."

"What?" he asked, his imagination supplying several possibilities. "Viper? Satan? Numero Uno?"

"Nothing quite that colorful. Just . . . Hunter." She fell silent for a moment, her fingers busily pleating and unpleating the hem of her shirt. "It's almost like fate, huh?"

TWO

Mallory arrived home Friday evening after a marathon session at the gym to find Evan's Lexus filling her parking spot. *What does he want?* she wondered, and waited for the familiar twist of pain. It didn't come. Curiosity, yes. A mild irritation, yes again. But pain? No. She breathed deeply of the chill night air, smiling to herself in the darkness. *Life goes on.*

The porch light lit up seconds before the front door flew open. "Mallory, where have you been? I've been waiting for hours." An unaccustomed frown knit Lindsey's brow. She advanced on her sister, her high heels clicking like castanets on the wooden boards of the entry deck.

"At least you didn't have to wait outside." Mallory frowned. "The funny thing is I don't remember leaving the door open."

Lindsey had the grace to look embarrassed. "You didn't. "I—"

"Found my spare key under the flowerpot." Mallory sighed. "I've got to come up with a better hiding place."

"Where have you been all this time?" Lindsey demanded, remembering her grievance.

"Well, maybe if you'd warned me you planned to stop by . . ."

"Mallory? Hellooo? What did you think I meant when I called this morning to see if you were busy after school?"

Oh, yeah. That call. "Sorry. I joined some fellow staff members to celebrate the official beginning of spring break, then headed straight for Aerobics Plus, where Hootie, the sadistic monster, tortured me in the name of physical fitness." Every muscle in her body ached. "By the way, could you have Evan move his car? He parked in my spot."

"Evan's not here. I borrowed the Lexus. I'll move it in a second, okay? I need you to do me a favor."

Another one? I already handed you my boyfriend on a silver platter. What more do you want? "Lindsey, I'm whipped. It's been a long day." Wearily, Mallory climbed the steps. All she wanted to do right now was take a shower, slip into her robe, and eat about six Symphony bars. The ones with toffee chips.

"But this is important!"

Mallory shot her sister a sharp sideways glance, alarmed at the quaver in her voice. "What's wrong?"

Lindsey's sophisticated facade dissolved in tears. "It's Evan," she wailed, loud enough to set every dog within a ten-block radius barking.

Wincing, Mallory ushered her inside, where Lindsey immediately threw herself on the sofa and burst into noisy sobs.

Mallory sighed in relief. If her sister was still indulging her flair for the dramatic, things couldn't be too serious.

Mallory tossed her jacket at the coatrack, then sinking into the familiar comfort of her big overstuffed armchair, kicked off her shoes and tucked her feet up under her. "What's the problem, Lindsey? What's Evan done?"

Lindsey sat up, brushing the tumbled blonde curls away from her face and batting tear-spiked eyelashes. "He's hiding something from me."

"Like what?"

She widened her big blue eyes. "I don't know, but I was hoping you'd help me find out."

Oh, no, thought Mallory. *I am not getting sucked into this one.* She shook her head from side to side.

Lindsey's expression shifted to a pout. "Please, Mallory."

"No."

"Just talk to him. He'll open up to you."

"No."

"Take him aside at the rehearsal dinner and see if you can get him to tell you what's going on. He's been getting all these long-distance phone calls lately. Something's up."

"What kind of something?" Mallory asked, her curiosity getting the better of her good judgment.

A spasm of embarrassment rippled across Lindsey's face. "Well, he cheated on you, didn't he?"

Did he? Mallory wondered. Can you cheat on someone you've never been intimate with in the first place? She shook her head again. "I can't help you, Linz. It's none of my business."

Lindsey's pout morphed into a phony smile, and Mallory braced herself for Act Two. "But Mal-lor-ree," Lindsey started, only to be interrupted by the simultaneous ringing of the telephone and the doorbell.

"Would you answer that?" Mallory nodded toward the portable phone on the table next to the sofa. "I'll get the door." She levered herself out of the chair and walked sock-footed across the room.

Lindsey answered the phone on the second ring. "Evan!" she said, sounding remarkably cheerful for someone who'd been in tears a few minutes earlier.

Distracted, Mallory swung the door open without checking the peephole first, then almost swallowed her tongue in surprise when she saw Brody Hunter filling her doorway. He shoved a pizza box at her. "I hope you like pepperoni."

The first thing to pop into her head was "Beware of Greeks bearing gifts," and it was out of her mouth before she had a chance to run it past her internal censor.

"Not applicable," he said. "I'm Romanian, remember?"

"See you soon, darling." Oblivious to Mallory and her visitor, Lindsey made kissing noises into the phone.

I may be sick. Mallory flicked a glance up at Brody and nearly laughed out loud at the expression on his face.

"The man-stealer?" he whispered.

She nodded, holding a finger to her lips. "Come on in," she said aloud. "I want you to meet my sister, Lindsey."

Lindsey, who had just put down the phone, glanced up at the mention of her name.

Mallory fought down an attack of the giggles sparked

by the dumbstruck expression on her sister's face. *Score one for my team!*

In a leather jacket and faded jeans, Brody Hunter looked handsome as the devil and just about as dangerous.

Lindsey struggled to her feet. "You're Hunter? You're the man Mallory's been dating?" Her voice was faint.

"In the flesh," he said.

And very nice flesh it was. Grinning, Mallory made the introductions.

Brody offered his hand. "Pleased to meet you. It's your wedding Mallory's dragging me to, right?"

Lindsey extended one limp hand and nodded mutely, still staring. They shook hands. Her sister appeared to be in shock. Mel Gibson himself couldn't have elicited a better reaction. Mallory grinned in satisfaction. *Poor Mallory, my foot.*

Brody released Lindsey's hand. A muscle twitched in her cheek, but she managed to muster a polite smile. "And how exactly did you two meet?"

In a gay bar, Mallory was sorely tempted to say, just to watch her sister's smile congeal.

She glanced sideways at Brody. A wicked grin curved his mouth, as if the same idea had occurred to him. Instead, he offered their agreed-upon cover story. "We ran into one another—literally—when Mallory was at police headquarters getting fingerprinted."

"Fingerprinted?" Pressing a hand to her throat, Lindsey turned to Mallory with a frown. "Why were you getting fingerprinted? You haven't been committing any crimes, have you?"

"No, all Oregon teachers have to be printed," Mallory explained. "It's the law." She set the pizza on the trunk.

"Really?" Lindsey raised an eyebrow, then glanced at Brody. "But you're no teacher. Why were you being fingerprinted?"

"I wasn't."

She narrowed her eyes in suspicion. "Then what were you doing at the police station?"

"Relax, Linz. He's a cop, not a crook. Detective. Does a lot of undercover work."

"I'm good at it too." Brody smiled. "The undercover work, I mean." He made himself at home on the love seat. "Got anything to drink, honey?"

It took Mallory a second or two to realize he was talking to her. "Milk or diet cola. They're both in the refrigerator. Help yourself."

Brody opened the pizza box and the savory odors of tomato sauce and Parmesan reminded Mallory just how hungry she was.

"I brought a large, so there's plenty. You're welcome to join us," he told Lindsey.

"No, I was just leaving. Thanks anyway. Walk me to the car, Mal?" It was more a demand than a question.

Mallory slipped her shoes on and followed Lindsey, pausing at the door to glance back at Brody. He winked, then added in a voice loud enough for Lindsey to overhear, "Don't be too long, honey. It's never as good when it's cold."

Lindsey clattered down the steps to the Lexus parked in the driveway. Once there, she whipped around to confront Mallory. "Are you sure that guy's a cop?"

Mallory laughed. "Yes, of course."

"There's no 'of course' about it!" Lindsey tapped

one foot in an impatient rhythm. "I've seen pictures of cold-blooded killers who looked less dangerous."

"With Brody, the only danger's the possibility of falling in love. A lousy idea, since he's not the marrying type."

"Marrying?" Lindsey gasped. "Marrying! Don't even think about it. Mother and Daddy would go ballistic if you brought home a man like that. I can see now why you've been so evasive."

Mallory wasn't the actress her sister was, but she managed a shamefaced look. "I guess my secret's out now." She heaved an exaggerated sigh. "But you have to admit he's gorgeous."

"If you go for the uncivilized macho-man type." Lindsey's expression made it clear that she didn't.

Not only had Brody retrieved a couple of glasses and a two-liter bottle of pop from the kitchen, he'd also finished his first slice of pizza and started on his second before Mallory made it back inside.

Her triumphant grin lit up the room as she closed the door behind her. "She bought it. 'Poor rejected, over-the-hill Mallory' just got upgraded to 'poor deluded, in-love-with-the-wrong-man Mallory.' "

"I'm the wrong man?" Brody did his best to look offended.

"Wrong for my family anyway." Mallory snagged a slice of pizza and settled back in the armchair. "Daddy's suspicious of anyone who wasn't born and raised in Brunswick, and my mother's prejudiced against men who have more hair than she does."

"Then I guess it's a good thing this is just a make-believe relationship." He poured a glass of pop and handed it to her.

"Thanks."

Again a fleeting smile lit her face, making him realize how solemn she looked most of the time. Why? Had her boyfriend's defection plunged her into a lingering depression? Or was her problem more complex?

None of your damn business, he reminded himself.

"What brings you here tonight, Brody?" Mallory's soft voice interrupted his thoughts.

He waved a slice of pizza. "I don't like to eat alone."

"I'm serious."

Yeah, so he'd noticed. "I thought we ought to spend some time together, get used to each other. Otherwise, we're going to have a tough time fooling anyone at the wedding."

"Meaning?"

"Yesterday you practically had a panic attack when I reached over to wipe a smudge of chocolate off your chin. If you react that way at the wedding, nobody's going to believe you're in love with me."

She fell silent, staring in apparent fascination at a string of mozzarella dangling from the lid of the pizza box like a miniature bungee cord. "My reaction had nothing to do with you. I'm just a person who needs a lot of personal space."

"But you want everyone to think we're involved, right?"

"That's the plan." She still wouldn't meet his gaze.

"Then I think we need to practice."

She looked up, startled. "Practice what?"

"Sitting side by side, for starters." He shrugged.

"We might be a little more believable as a couple if you didn't flinch whenever I come within five feet of you."

"I don't flinch."

"Oh, no?" He moved to her side and leaned casually against the arm of her chair.

She shrank away like a turtle retreating into its shell.

Brody stepped back, folding his arms across his chest. "I rest my case." He returned to the love seat and helped himself to another slice of pizza.

"No fair. You startled me."

"Exactly my point."

She lifted her chin. Her gaze was direct and unwavering, her mouth a tight line of determination, but the rapid rise and fall of her chest betrayed her true state of mind.

"I'm no threat to you," he said.

"I know that."

"You don't react this way to Kyle."

"No, but . . ."

"What?"

"I've known Kyle a long time. I barely know you at all."

"Then you'd better get to know me. Otherwise this isn't going to work. Not if you shy like a nervous horse every time I get close. Come sit by me." He patted the space next to him on the love seat. "I don't bite. Think of me as someone harmless, an older brother, a favorite uncle, the boy next door."

She froze, her eyes wide and blank.

"Mallory?" What had he said now?

She blinked twice, then slowly focused her gaze on him. "I'm being silly, huh?"

"Not silly. Cautious. And with weirdos like GI Joe running around loose, some caution is in order."

"But you're not GI Joe."

"No." Though he damned well wished he knew who was. "Did you ever play make-believe games when you were a kid?"

"All the time."

"Well, that's what this is. Make-believe. All you have to do is pretend to be interested in me."

"Like you're pretending to be interested in me?"

"Right," he said, though he wasn't sure as he gazed into her eyes if he was pretending or not. Despite her hang-ups, Mallory Scott was a very appealing woman, more so perhaps because she seemed totally unaware of how attractive she was.

Smiling nervously, she sat down next to him. Her breathing was rapid. Her hands shook.

Brody gave her an encouraging look. "Don't hyper-ventilate. Just relax."

She shut her eyes and her breathing slowed, but her hands still trembled.

Brody kept his voice low. "Okay, Mallory, I'm going to put my arm around your shoulders. Try not to tighten up."

She made an obvious effort to relax, but her shoulder felt as rigid as a board under his hand. Maybe that was the problem. Her effort was obvious.

"This isn't working," he said. "Open your eyes. Let's play the 'what if' game."

She eyed him uncertainly. "I don't know that one."

"It's easy. I pose a question. You answer off the top of your head. Ready? What if you won ten million dollars?"

She grinned. "I'd retire to Tahiti. How about you?"

"I'd quit my job to train full-time for the Olympics."

"In what sport?"

"All of 'em. I dream big." He squeezed her shoulders. She tensed, but only for a second. "Okay, second question. What if aliens took over the earth?"

"Aliens?" She laughed. "I'd cancel their green cards and send them back to their home world. What would you do?"

"Me? Well, since I have it on authority that aliens are allergic to tropical breezes, I guess I'd retire to Tahiti."

"No fair! Think up your own answer." She leaned forward to scoop up a slice of pizza. Brody, who'd had the same idea, was a fraction of a second slower. Her hand closed on the pizza and his hand closed on hers. Mallory stiffened again and uttered a nearly inaudible gasp.

As her startled gaze met his Brody murmured an involuntary, "Oh!" Which didn't fall under the heading of witty repartee, but then, the unexpected physical contact seemed to have short-circuited his brain.

"Brody?" she whispered, looking as confused as he felt. Her fingers trembled in his.

"Hmm?" He blinked, fighting to clear his head. For some reason, he couldn't seem to think and look into her eyes at the same time, a circumstance he found unsettling. Very unsettling. A man could drown himself in the depths of those eyes.

"Brody?" she repeated in a shaky voice. "Is this part of the game?" She dropped the pizza and tugged her fingers free of his, breaking the spell.

"What?" He stood abruptly. "Part of the game? No, I think the game's over for tonight." He cleared his throat. "I just remembered I promised someone I'd do something."

Mallory's face went blank. Then she shifted her gaze, veiling her expression behind a thick fringe of eyelashes.

Oh, great. Now he'd hurt her feelings. And no wonder. *I promised someone I'd do something.* Talk about pitiful excuses.

Mallory rose. Her cheeks were faintly pink, but she looked him right in the eye. "I'm sorry if I offended you, Brody. Of course it was part of the game. I never really meant to question your motives. It's just . . ." She dropped her gaze. "I keep forgetting. I mean, you don't seem . . ."

Gay? Good reason for that. He took a deep breath. *I should tell her,* he thought. But then she'd never be able to relax enough to carry off the charade. And Kyle had told him how important this was to her. Hell, another week and he'd be out of her life forever. Surely he could keep his mouth shut and his hormones in check that long.

"Brody?"

He looked at her. Big mistake.

She captured his right hand in hers and gave him a formal handshake. "Thanks for dinner. I really appreciate what you're doing for me."

Yeah, but did she have any idea what she was doing for him?

No, he decided, she didn't have a clue. Her eyes were wide and guileless, her soft pink lips curved in an innocent smile. God, but he was tempted to kiss her. What could it hurt?

Unfortunately, he didn't have a chance to find out, because his beeper went off. "May I use your phone?"

She nodded and handed him the portable.

"GI Joe?" Her voice shook.

"Either him or the damn burglary ring," he muttered as he punched in the number for the police department.

"I read about them in the *Gazette*. They've hit a dozen places in the last few months."

"Yeah, the robberies started right after I moved down here." The dispatcher answered and transferred him to Officer Armstrong.

"Got another one for you, Detective."

Regan Armstrong always made *detective* sound like a dirty word. From what he'd observed, she was a good cop, but no one would nominate her for Miss Congeniality.

"Big house at 1508 Chisholm Drive. Owner's been out of town on business. Just got back tonight to find he'd been robbed. They took jewelry, cash, guns, electronic equipment. The usual."

"I'll be right there."

Mallory munched at the slice of cold pizza Brody had left behind and indulged in a little introspection, an activity she normally avoided as assiduously as she avoided Mrs. Gooding, her proselytizing next-door neighbor.

Brody Hunter confused her, something men usually didn't do. If they were "safe" men like her dad or Kyle or Evan, she treated them pretty much the same way she did women. And if they were "dangerous" men like a couple of the oversexed testosterone factories who hung out at Aerobics Plus, she simply kept her distance. No confusion there.

But Brody was different. He acted safe, but she *re*-acted as if he were dangerous, and she couldn't figure out why. She knew he wasn't going to make a move on her, yet for a second, when she was shaking his hand and thanking him for his help, she'd thought he was about to kiss her, a prospect that should have terrified her. But didn't. And that was the most confusing part of all.

"Rise and shine!" Kyle, the morning person.

Mallory grunted into the phone.

"That's your imitation of a pig, right?"

"Good grief, Kyle. How can you be so cheerful at"—she peered nearsightedly at the digital alarm clock on her bedside table—"six-oh-seven in the morning?"

"You don't want to be late, do you?"

"Late for what?" she asked, her voice heavy with suspicion.

"I took the liberty of scheduling some appointments for you."

Great. After two days of conferencing with parents at school, all she needed were a few more appointments. "What kind of appointments?"

"For starters, you're going to get your hair and nails done at Mr. Edouard's. Then a facial, a session in the tanning booth, and a bikini wax at Kiki's."

"Nix the bikini wax. I'm going to a wedding, not posing for the swimsuit issue of *Sports Illustrated*."

"But it's free. Kiki tossed it in as a bonus. With summer coming, her girls need the practice."

"Let them practice on somebody else!"

"Okay, okay. If you're adamant, we'll scratch the bikini wax."

"Great. Mr. Edouard followed by Kiki. That's going to take all morning."

"Pretty much. We can shop this afternoon."

"Shop?"

"For a dress. You don't intend to wear pants to the rehearsal dinner, do you?"

Actually, she had planned to do just that. "What's wrong with pants?"

"They don't show off your legs, and your legs are one of your best assets."

"They are?" Mallory flipped the covers aside and examined the appendages in question. They were okay. No cellulite and only a few stubbly patches she'd missed with her razor.

"So? What do you say?"

"I don't know, Kyle. I haven't bought a dress in a while. No need for one. Slacks are more practical for work, especially when I have playground duty."

"Come on, Mallory. Be impractical for once in your life."

She grinned at the telephone receiver. Kyle didn't have a clue how truly impractical she could be. He'd never seen the contents of her underwear drawer. "Okay, you're on."

"You won't regret it, Cinderella. By the way, did I mention we're meeting Brody for lunch so you two can iron out the final details of your dates?"

Lunch with Brody. Suddenly Mallory wasn't sleepy anymore.

THREE

Brody was saving a booth for them. She spotted him through the window of the diner as Kyle pulled into a parking spot. *The man is gay.* Funny how she had to keep reminding herself.

His broad shoulders and muscular arms showed to advantage in a blue knit shirt. Add to that a killer smile and he was enough to set any woman's heart aflutter.

The lethal smile put in a sudden appearance as he caught sight of them, and Mallory's heart shifted into overdrive.

"Brody's here already," she told Kyle, then blinked in surprise at the rush she felt just saying his name. "I thought you said he was habitually late."

Kyle grunted. "He is. That's why I told him to meet us at a quarter to twelve."

Mallory got out on the passenger's side. "But it's a quarter after."

"Right. Listen, I've got to run a quick errand. Just order me a BLT and coffee, would you?"

She hung on to the door handle as if it were a life-line. "You're not coming in?" Mallory was proud of the fact that her panic wasn't reflected in her voice.

"I'll be right back. I have to drop off some stuff at the cleaners."

She wanted to offer to accompany Kyle just so she didn't have to face Brody alone. He's no threat, she told herself. Intellectually, she acknowledged the fact, but emotionally . . .

Not all men were boy-next-door types. And just because a man looked dangerous, it didn't mean he was. Mallory took one deep, calming breath. Then she slammed the door shut, waved Kyle off, and turned toward the diner.

Porky's had been a fixture in Brunswick since before Mallory was born. Though it was popular nowadays with all age groups, it had started in the fifties as a teen hang-out.

Mallory felt a little like a teenager herself, as insecure as if she were on her first date. *The guy is doing you a favor, Mallory. He has no expectations. Zero. So relax.*

"Hi." He met her at the door, looking so pleased to see her that her heart did a couple of cartwheels.

"Hi, yourself." She smiled slowly, her nervousness forgotten as their gazes met and held for a long moment. "Kyle will be here in a minute. He had an errand to run."

"I saved us a booth. This way." He ushered her down the narrow aisle, one hand at the small of her back.

Her skin tingled at the contact.

They had barely taken their places on the red plastic benches across from one another when a hair-netted middle-aged waitress showed up, a stub of a pencil poised above her order pad.

"There will be three of us altogether," Mallory told her. "Another friend will be joining us shortly."

"Separate checks?"

Mallory looked at Brody.

He grinned. "Nah. The friend invited us. We'll stick him with the bill."

Mallory laughed. "Sounds fair to me."

They placed their orders and the waitress moved on.

Mallory took a sip of water, a stalling tactic while she tried to think of something to say. "Did you catch the burglars last night?"

He made a disgusted noise. "I wish."

"No leads?"

"Not a one. I didn't honestly expect any. These guys are slick operators. Fourteen robberies to date, but we don't have a clue who's pulling the jobs. No fingerprints, no eyewitnesses. We can't even figure how they're fencing the stuff. And as if that weren't enough to run us ragged, we've got that damn rapist to nail. Five victims we know of. And probably twice that many who haven't come forward." He broke off abruptly. "But enough of my frustrations. What's happening at school these days?"

Mallory struggled to keep her face calm, her voice even. "Not much. We're on spring break."

Brody's pager went off, and a rueful expression crossed his face. "Wish cops got spring breaks." He stood. "I'll be right back. I've got to call in."

The diner was filling up rapidly. The murmur of the customers' voices competed with Travis Tritt on the jukebox and the frequent call of "Order up!" from the kitchen.

Sipping her water, Mallory studied her reflection in the stainless-steel napkin holder. She looked fine. Reassuringly normal. Gradually, her heart rate slowed and the panic subsided.

In fact, if you discounted the distortions caused by the slight curve of the metal surface, she looked better than normal, which was good news since she'd been a little dubious about the notoriously scissor-happy Mr. Edouard. But between him and Kiki, she'd turned out all right. At least no one had screamed and run at the sight of her yet.

"Mallory?"

She whipped her head around at the sound of a familiar voice. *Evan.* She hadn't talked to him face-to-face once since he and Lindsey had announced their engagement. She wasn't prepared for this. Not now. Apprehension was a cold knot in her chest. Where the heck were Kyle and Brody?

Evan Corby, handsome as ever, smiled his winsome, little-boy smile. "How have you been? Haven't seen much of you lately."

What did he expect? She sighed. "Have a seat."

Instead of sliding into the booth on Brody's side, he squeezed in next to her, capturing her hands between his own. "You're coming to the rehearsal dinner, aren't you?"

She nodded. "Lindsey would put out a contract on me if I tried to skip out."

"Good." He gave her hands a little squeeze, smiling tenderly. "I've missed you."

Confused, Mallory studied their entwined hands.

They'd never held hands before. Why start now? Lindsey was right. He was acting strangely. "Evan," she started uncertainly, "what's going on?"

"Nothing. I'm just happy to see you."

Mallory tried to tug her hands free, but he tightened his grip. She frowned. "I, on the other hand, am not particularly happy to see you. Have you forgotten the fact that you dumped me flat after eleven years? That you didn't even have the decency to tell me yourself? That I had to hear the news of your engagement from my mother?"

"Mallory," he coaxed, employing the same smile he'd used to con her into cleaning his apartment, walking his dog, and picking out his mother's Christmas present. "Don't be angry. I couldn't help falling in love with Lindsey. I didn't plan it. In fact, I'd always assumed that someday we'd . . ." He let it trail off, then sighed deeply. "A part of me will always love you."

Right. The same way she loved her comfy old blue sweats with the hole in the knee.

Evan's gaze probed hers. "Friends?"

"Gee golly, I hope so," drawled Brody.

Mallory glanced up in surprise at the sound of his voice. He was smiling, but his eyes held a glint of steel.

"Otherwise I'm going to have to beat the living daylights out of you, mister. Hands off." This time the menace was unmistakable.

Evan dropped her fingers as if they'd burned him and smiled at Brody like a man who was auditioning for a toothpaste commercial. "I—uh . . ." For once, the silver-tongued anchorman was at a loss for words.

Ignoring him, Brody slid into the booth and reached

across the Formica table to trace the line of her cheek-bone with his thumb. "Sorry I took so long, honey."

Damn, he was good. She glanced at Evan to see if he was buying it, but she couldn't tell for sure. His face was frozen in the ingratiating-smile position. Either he didn't know quite what to make of Brody Hunter or he was scared spitless. Maybe both.

"Was your call bad news?"

"The worst, dammit. I've got to run." Cupping her jaw, Brody rubbed the pad of his thumb across her lower lip. "Will you miss me?"

Even though she knew the whole thing was part of an act put on for Evan's benefit, she trembled in reaction. "Desperately."

"I'll miss you too." He smiled into her eyes, kissed the tip of his index finger, and pressed it against her mouth.

Mallory sighed. Good? He was great.

After one last lingering look, Brody stood, then turned to Evan, offering a hand. "Brody Hunter. Don't believe I caught your name."

Evan blinked. "Corby. Evan Corby."

"Right. You're the one who's engaged to Mallory's sister."

"And you're Hunter, you say? Then that makes you Mallory's . . ." He paused as if he weren't quite sure how to fill in the blank. Boyfriend? Date? Lover?

"Yeah." Brody's voice was husky. "Mallory's. All Mallory's." He captured her hand, pressing a kiss to her wrist.

Mallory's eyelids fluttered shut and she gave an involuntary shiver. Great? He was flat out incredible.

Evan muttered something she didn't quite catch, still preoccupied as she was with Brody's amazing technique.

"Mallory?" Brody's voice was a raspy whisper, as intimate as a caress.

She shivered again. "Hmm?"

"He's gone."

"Gone?" Mallory lifted her heavy eyelids to see Evan disappearing through the archway that led to the dining room.

"Yes, and I've got to go too. But we still have things to discuss. What say we get together again tonight?"

Was he asking her out on a real date? More important, did she want him to ask her out on a real date? She did. Unfortunately . . . "I can't. I promised my mother I'd show up there for dinner. She's having some of the relatives over."

He raised an eyebrow. "To honor the happy couple?"

She nodded.

"On the entertainment scale, I'd rank that right up there with an infomercial marathon."

She laughed. "It won't be that bad. Aunt Chloe talks too much, but Uncle Toby's fun. The only part I dread is dealing with the whispers and sympathetic looks. You'd swear Lindsey had stolen my last functioning kidney instead of my boyfriend."

"What if you brought a date? Would your relatives see you in a different light then?"

"Oh, Brody, that would solve everything. But I can't ask you to do it."

"You didn't ask. I'm offering. Think of it as a dry run for the wedding. What time should I pick you up?"

"Seven?"

"I'll be there. And Mallory . . . ?"

She tipped her face up expectantly.

He leaned down, shoved her glasses back up to the bridge of her nose, and brushed her lips with his.

The light pressure of his mouth barely qualified as a kiss, but it was enough to send her blood pressure soaring. Her heart raced. Heat enveloped her. Yet somehow, in the midst of all the physical turmoil, her confusion evaporated. She stared at Brody and saw the truth in a moment of crystal clarity.

"You're not gay." The words emerged in a nearly inaudible whisper.

Brody smiled and her poor, overworked heart skipped a beat. "No, I'm not. See you tonight."

Dumbfounded, she watched him saunter to the door. The man practically oozed testosterone; she wasn't the only woman in the diner with her eyes glued to his backside. Why had she believed for one second that he was gay?

Because of Kyle, she realized. And speak of the devil . . .

Kyle strolled in just as Brody was leaving. They exchanged a few words and Kyle shot her a wary look.

You should be leery, old buddy. While they shopped for the perfect dress this afternoon, she intended to chew him up one side and down the other.

Brody rang Mallory's doorbell at a quarter to eight. He'd been running a little behind all day.

"You're late," she said in lieu of hello.

"Sorry. Time got away from me." He smiled.

She didn't smile back. She didn't ask him in, either.

She just stood there in the doorway, staring at him as if he were something that had oozed up out of the sewer. Doggone it, she wasn't just irritated. She was mad. Nail-spitting, tooth-gnashing, foot-stomping, ass-chewing mad.

On to Plan B. He pumped up the wattage on his grin. Times like this he could use a nice set of dimples.

"For you," he said, and presented her with an armful of red carnations. The way he figured it, she'd be less likely to deck him if her hands were full.

She frowned. "Thanks. But if you think a few flowers are going to get you off the hook, then you'd better think again."

"I should have called."

"Yes, you should have."

"In a way I'm glad I didn't, though, or I'd have missed this."

She raised an eyebrow. "Missed what?"

"Your temper. You're damned cute when you're ticked off."

Her expression fluctuated between pleasure and irritation before finally leveling off somewhere around tolerance. She stepped back out of the doorway with an exasperated sigh. "You may as well come in."

He walked across the threshold, waving a box of chocolate-covered macadamia nuts like a white flag. "Just in case the flowers didn't get me through the door," he explained, and was rewarded by a reluctant chuckle.

"You're a—"

"Man in a million?" he suggested.

"Sure. If that's a synonym for pain in the rear." Mallory buried her face in the flowers, breathing deeply. "I guess you're off the hook, though. Carnations are my favorites."

They'd been Jenna's favorites too. "I thought they might be. You remind me of someone I used to know, someone who loved carnations."

"Someone you cared about?" Those eyes of hers saw too much.

"Yeah." He didn't want to talk about Jenna, so he laid the candy on Mallory's trunk-slash-coffee table and forced a smile. "We'd better get going. I'd hate to make a bad first impression."

"Too late. When I called my mother fifteen minutes ago to tell her we'd been unavoidably detained, she muttered something about curdled hollandaise and rude, ungrateful guests. The woman is not a happy camper. Maybe you ought to save the flowers to pacify her."

"Got it covered. Hers are in the Jeep."

Mallory shot him a calculating look. "Sounds like you've had a lot of practice soothing ruffled feathers."

"Some," he admitted. "Shall we go? I'd hate to miss dessert."

"Just let me take care of the flowers first. Even if they are just a guilt offering, they're beautiful, Brody. Thank you."

She moved with a graceful economy of motion, arranging the carnations in a cut-glass vase, filling it with water, then collecting her coat and purse.

"Ready?" he asked, taking her arm.

If he hadn't been looking for it, he wouldn't have noticed her slight flinch. But she recovered quickly. The next instant a teasing smile tilted the corners of her mouth. "*I've* been ready for ages."

He pressed one hand to his chest in mock pain. "I thought you said I was off the hook."

"That just means your transgression's forgiven, not forgotten." She flipped on the outside lights and locked the front door. Then they walked side by side toward his Jeep. He liked the feel of her next to him, soft and warm and feminine.

"That's odd." She paused on the curb.

"What is?" Brody hoped she wasn't referring to the abnormally rapid cadence of his breathing. Touching her—even touching her through all those layers of clothing—triggered some pretty powerful responses.

"There's a light on at the Yanos'." She gestured toward the house across the street.

"It's dark out, Mallory. People generally do turn on the lights at night."

She steered him across the pavement, avoiding a pothole half-full of water. "Not when they're on vacation in Barbados."

He placed his hand over hers. "You realize it's probably just someone who's come in to feed the cats and water the plants?"

"They don't have any cats. And I'm the one they asked to water the plants. I'm the one with the spare key." She dug it out of her bag.

"This isn't very smart," Brody protested. "If it's some other friend or relative, you're going to feel like a fool, and if it's a burglar, you'd be smarter to call the cops."

"Hey, Brody!"

"What?"

"*You're* a cop. Consider yourself called." With a nimble twist of her supple body, she slipped from his restraining grip and dashed across her neighbors' lawn.

Brody damned near tripped over the curb trying to catch up. He grabbed her arm, forcing her to a halt on the front step. "Look, this is no joke. If you suspect wrongdoing, let the professionals handle it. Don't put yourself in danger."

She stared expressionlessly at his hand on her arm. Her body quivered almost imperceptibly, as if she fought a private battle there in the shadows.

Brody couldn't tell what she was thinking, but he suspected it had little to do with the lights at her neighbors' house. Depths. Oh, yes. The lady had depths.

Suddenly Mallory cocked her head to one side. "Did you hear that? Someone's moving around inside."

"I heard it," he whispered. "And whoever's inside is going to hear us if you don't lower your voice." He tightened his grip on her arm, half-afraid she'd use her key to sneak inside if he let her go.

"What should we do?"

"Not one damn thing without backup. Go call nine-one-one. I'll keep an eye on things here."

The lights went out, and he swore under his breath, pulling Mallory into the deeper shadows behind a bushy mugho pine.

The door opened a cautious inch at a time, and a man emerged. A big man. A bulldozer of a man. Taller than Brody and a good eighty pounds heavier. He probed the shadows with a flashlight. "Nobody out here," he called to someone in the house. "Must have been your imagination." He retreated into the house, closing the door quietly behind him.

"Big boy, huh?" Brody whispered. "Could you see his face?"

Mallory shook her head. "No, and I'm betting the Yanos never have, either. Should I call nine-one-one now?"

He nodded. "Tell the dispatcher Detective Hunter's on the scene requesting backup on a possible burglary attempt. Give the address and tell them no sirens."

"Got it."

Brody gave her hand a final squeeze of encouragement, and she slipped back across the street.

As soon as she was gone, he realized his mistake. He should have asked that the backup come down the alley. Since his Jeep was the only vehicle parked along the street the entire length of the block, it stood to reason the burglars must have parked in the alley. So obviously, they wouldn't be leaving by the front door.

The backyard was fenced. Brody eyed the seven-foot-high cedar obstacle in dismay. Damn, he hated fences. Ought to be a city ordinance against them. Every time he tackled one, he either tore his clothes to shreds or pulled a muscle in his back.

Oh, well. Maybe this time would be an exception. He took a running start and vaulted over the top.

So much for exceptions. Although his clothing and muscles survived intact for a change, he damn near gelded himself when he landed in a lilac bush.

Grunting and swearing under his breath, he staggered to his feet. Dammit to hell and back, he hoped they hadn't heard his crash landing inside the house. A hope, he soon realized, doomed to disappointment.

The French doors onto the deck flew open and two

dark-clad figures emerged at a run. One of them tripped over the barbecue grill, stifling a curse.

Brody didn't see any weapons on display, but since he wasn't armed himself, confrontation didn't seem like the wisest move. Not when the odds were two to one in their favor. Damn near three to one, considering the size of the guy who'd peeked out the front door earlier.

The burglars took off across the yard at a fast clip. No time now to wait for backup.

Hugging the shadows and nursing his damaged equipment, he followed the muffled noise of their retreat to the back gate. Moving at top limping speed, he stumbled into the alley just in time to see a vehicle running without lights turn right onto Park Boulevard.

Damn. Double damn. Too dark to read the license plate. But as the bulky vehicle turned onto the lighted street, he realized it was a pickup, a late-model two-tone gray Ford with a matching canopy.

"Let me get this straight, Hunter." Regan Armstrong's grin set his teeth on edge.

She had cornered him at the coffee machine. Mallory was in the police station's reception area, rereading the transcript of her statement.

"You stumble onto a robbery in progress, our first real lead in the case, then instead of waiting for backup, you hop the fence, making enough noise in the process to alert the burglars. Then, while you're standing around with your thumb up your butt, they make a clean escape. And you don't even get the license number of the getaway vehicle. Smooth move, hotshot."

"What brings you downtown this time of night, Regan? You're not on duty."

"Stopped by to check next week's duty schedule." She raised an eyebrow, folding her arms across her chest. "You wouldn't be trying to change the subject, would you, Detective?"

"Hell, no. I wouldn't dream of it. What can I tell you?"

She gave him a speculative look. "To start with, you might explain what were you doing in that part of town."

"Picking me up. We were on our way to dinner." Mallory, having survived her brush with bureaucracy, had come looking for Brody. "And if you'll excuse us, we're late."

"Nice save," said Brody as soon as they were safely out of earshot. "Thanks."

"That woman doesn't seem to like you much."

"Officer Armstrong doesn't like anybody much."

"But especially you."

"Yeah." He shrugged. "She's got it in for me because I got her promotion. At least that's her view of the situation. Personally, I don't think the chief would have made her detective even if I hadn't been in the picture."

"Why? Because she's a woman?" Brody could practically see Mallory's feminist hackles rise.

"No, because she's erratic and unpredictable. Officer Armstrong runs through partners the way a hay-fever sufferer runs through tissues, the way the Highlander runs through evil immortals, the way Liz Taylor runs through husbands, the way—"

Mallory held up one hand like a traffic cop. "Enough

already. I get it." She stopped next to his Jeep. "What time is it, anyway? I'm starving."

"Five after ten."

"That late? No wonder Mother was so snippy on the phone."

"I'm sorry."

"Not your fault this time." She shrugged. "Who knew giving a statement would take that long?"

She looked so depressed, he pulled her into his arms and hugged her close.

Despite his earlier experiences with her abnormal responses, he wasn't prepared for her reaction. Mallory didn't flinch or jerk away this time. Instead, she went very still and stiff, as if she'd suddenly turned to stone. Or ice.

He could feel her body close to his, smell the faint, citrusy fragrance of her perfume, hear her quick, gasping respirations. But her eyes were empty, as if her spirit had retreated to some secret inner sanctum. Fear prickled along the back of his neck. "Mallory? What's wrong?"

She blinked and her eyes came back into focus. "Nothing." She stepped away from him, putting a careful distance between them. Her laughter sounded a false note. "I'm just tired. Please take me home."

"Why? What's the problem? Did I do something to make you angry?"

"I'm not angry."

"You look angry."

"I told you. I'm tired."

"A minute ago you said you were hungry. How about we drop by Denny's and grab something? They're open all night."

"Sorry, Brody. I just don't feel like it."

"We could get some takeout if you'd rather."

"No thanks."

Confused, he studied her. She wouldn't even look at him. Kyle had said she had a problem relating to men. Obviously, she didn't like being touched. Yet earlier, at the diner, she hadn't shied away from him. Of course, that had been make-believe, part of their "act." At Porky's, she'd been concentrating on convincing her ex-boyfriend she wasn't nursing a broken heart. And at Porky's, he suddenly realized, she'd still been thinking of him as Kyle's friend, a nice, nonthreatening homosexual. Now she knew the truth.

"Mallory?" He pitched his voice low.

"What?"

"You know our little charade isn't going to convince anyone if you go catatonic every time I touch you."

"I know, but—"

"Look at me."

She stared into his eyes, her face expressionless, remote.

"What's the problem?"

"I don't really know you, Brody."

He studied her taut features. "It's more than that."

She swallowed audibly. "Like I told you before, I'm the sort of person who needs a lot of personal space. It takes me a while to warm up to people."

To men, she meant. Somebody, somewhere along the line, must have inflicted some pretty serious damage. The tightly controlled muscles of her face, the rigid set of her shoulders, awakened protective instincts he hadn't even realized he possessed. "I would never hurt you."

She was silent for a long time. When she finally

spoke, he had to lean close to hear her whispered reply. "Not on purpose anyway."

Depths. Deep, dark, murky depths. Mallory's expression remained stolid and unresponsive, but her hands were balled into fists and her eyes were clouded with pain.

Brody stared at the thick black shadows puddled along the base of the two-story city-hall building and pretended her distress didn't bother him. A sharp wind rustled the dead cheat grass edging the parking lot. Traffic sounds ebbed and flowed sporadically, governed by the light at the corner of College Boulevard and Northwest Fourth.

Mallory sighed softly.

The faint sound sent another unexpected wave of protectiveness surging over Brody. He shivered, denying the validity of such an alien sensation. *You don't need this crap*, he told himself. *You barely know the woman. Her problems have nothing to do with you. You're Brody "Let's Not Get Too Serious, Baby" Hunter, and you don't give a rat's behind what's worrying this screwed-up female.*

Only problem was, he did care. In fact, he found Mallory's reactions deeply disturbing. Why did she respond so violently to a casual touch? Had some sadistic bastard abused her in the past? Was that why she was so touchy? Why she kept men at a distance? The possibility bugged the hell out of him.

He glanced over at her. She stood huddled in her coat, face averted from his. She looked so small and fragile. He wanted to cradle her in his arms, rock her and hold her and tell her everything was going to be all right, but he suspected if he did, he'd only frighten her. He rammed his hands deep in his pockets.

The wind gusted suddenly, tipping over one of the

plastic garbage cans lined up along the back of the apartment complex across the alley. The heavier trash spread out in a fan shape, but the wind caught the lighter items. A flurry of papers headed their way. One of them, the stained and crumpled front page of last Monday's *Gazette*, wrapped itself around his legs. He reached down to free himself and froze. Even upside down, the headline read like an omen sent by a malicious oracle. GI JOE AT-TACKS ANOTHER HAPLESS VICTIM.

Dammit all, was that it? He tasted bile. Dear God, just like Jenna.

Brody shivered again, belatedly realizing the front blowing in had turned the night cold. "We should be going." His breath emerged in puffs of frozen water vapor. "You must be freezing."

She nodded, her movements stiff and graceless. "My poor legs feel like Popsicles." Her self-deprecating laughter sounded almost natural.

Brody unlocked the passenger door of his Jeep. He started to help her in, but remembering the unwritten ground rules just in time, he hastily pulled his hand away.

FOUR

Mallory spotted the Lexus parked in front of her house from a block and a half away. Lindsey had no doubt helped herself to the key under the flowerpot again. Maybe she'd even dragged Evan along. Great. Two of the three people—her mother being the third—Mallory most wished to avoid.

"I changed my mind," she told Brody. "I would like to get something to eat, after all."

"Yeah?"

"Absolutely!" Did her enthusiasm sound as false to his ears as it did to hers?

He paused at the stop sign. "Why?"

"Why what?"

"Why the sudden change of heart? And don't give me that stuff about a woman's prerogative."

He sounded more curious than angry, which was a miracle. She'd figured he was probably sick to death of her and her moods by now. The problem was, she was beginning to like Brody Hunter. A lot. And that wasn't part of the plan. Because she had nothing to offer him, nothing but a truckload of frustration.

What should she tell him? What could she tell him? *Well, when you hugged me in the parking lot back there, I freaked for a minute. But I'm okay now, and the fact is I'd rather spend more time with you than have to deal with my sister or my ex-boyfriend.*

She sighed. When in doubt, tell the truth. Or at least part of it. "Evan's car is parked in front of my house. See it? The black Lexus?" She shrugged. "I don't know if it's Evan or Lindsey or both of them. I just know I'm not in the mood to talk to them right now."

"Maybe they heard about your run-in with the burglars. Maybe they're worried."

"I doubt it. Curious perhaps. Evan has a nose for news and Lindsey's just plain snoopy. So either they want to give me the third degree about my evening's adventure or they've had a tiff and want me to play Dear Abby." She leaned her head back against her headrest. "I really don't want to deal with them tonight."

"Then don't." A smile spread slowly across his face, warming her. He did a quick U-turn and headed back toward the business section of town.

The Denny's out by the freeway didn't serve haute cuisine, but aside from the Hitchin' Post where the bikers hung out and a couple of all-night convenience stores patronized by insomniacs and weirdos, it was the only place open. Brody hung a left onto the access road, then a right into the parking area. The front lot was full, but there were some empty spots around the side.

As he pulled in he noticed a late-model gray Ford

pickup with matching camper parked near the Dumpster. Probably not the same one he'd seen leaving the alley behind the Yanos', but worth checking out on the off chance.

"Gotta go wash up," he told Mallory as soon as the hostess showed them to a table. No use worrying her. It was probably nothing anyway. No doubt a town this size had two dozen trucks that fit the description. Maybe more. "If the waitress comes to take the order before I get back, tell her I want a cheeseburger, fries, and a chocolate shake. Okay?"

Mallory nodded.

The bathrooms opened off a short hall between the restaurant and the lounge. At the far end a glowing neon exit sign indicated the location of the back door. Brushing past a teenage girl using one of the pay phones, he slipped outside.

A gust of wind blew grit in his eyes. *Jeez.* He tucked his ponytail into his jacket and pulled the collar up around his neck. *Spring break, my foot.* That wind was straight off a glacier.

He detoured around the Dumpster to where the truck was parked. With one of the security lights out, the area was darker than six inches up a cat's behind. He had to hunker down and squint like hell to read the license number. It was one of the standard Oregon plates, navy blue on a pale background with a green pine tree separating letters and numbers. "L-R-K—" Brody leaned closer, but before he could decipher the numbers, his head exploded in pain and all the lights went out.

❖———————❖

Mallory checked her watch for the third time in ten minutes. According to Mickey Mouse, Brody Hunter had just qualified for the *Guinness Book of World Records* in the "longest time spent washing hands" category.

Mallory added another shredded napkin to the pile in front of her. Where the heck was he? The waitress had taken their order twenty minutes ago. Other customers—numerous other customers—had come and gone. Mallory was tempted to follow suit. Not only was she sick and tired of waiting, she was also beginning to feel conspicuous sitting here by herself.

Kyle had assured her this little black dress was the epitome of chic, but she was beginning to wonder. Two guys had hit on her already and the state police officer at the counter was keeping his eye on her, and being pretty obvious about it too. Getting booked on suspicion of prostitution was not the way she wanted to finish up her evening.

In the lounge, a whiny female vocalist was destroying a perfectly good Billy Joel song. Even muffled by distance, the nasal quality of her voice grated on Mallory's nerves. Dammit, where was Brody?

She drained her water glass and started on her diet soda. Half an hour. Ridiculous. Was the men's room out of soap? Water? What? This wasn't a date. It was a nightmare. The upside was, things couldn't get much worse.

Or could they?

A John Travolta wannabe in black leather and chains swaggered through the front door. Mallory's heart plummeted. Ramon, the loser from Dial-A-Date.

He spotted her immediately. "Mallory! Babe, how's it going?" he yelled across the room.

Mallory prayed for the earth to open up and swallow her.

It didn't.

Ramon slithered toward her, his arrival heralded by the stench of cheap cologne. He grabbed her hand and for one horrified moment she thought he was going to kiss it, but all he did was give it a squeeze, then let it drop. "Babe, how are you?"

"Fine."

He raised the left half of his single eyebrow. "Don't lie to Ramon, babe. What's going on? Date stand you up?"

"He'll be right back." He'd *better* be right back.

"I get it. Hitting the little boys' room, hmm?" He sat down across from her, uninvited. "Listen, babe, you get tired of waiting for Romeo, you head on into the lounge. I got a friend lined up in there, one of my regulars, a real party animal. You're welcome to join us. No charge." He winked suggestively. "The more the merrier, you know?"

Mallory didn't know, and she was quite certain she didn't want to know. She frowned at the little toad. Subtlety was wasted on his type. "Get lost, Ramon."

"Now, babe, you're gonna hurt my feelings if you're not careful."

"Is there a problem here?" asked the patrolman from the counter. He was short, stocky, and middle-aged, but he looked like a knight in shining armor to Mallory.

"No, sir. No problem here, sir." Ramon sounded like the painfully polite sleazoid perpetrators on *Cops*.

"Yes," Mallory said. "I have a problem."

Ramon shoved his chair back. "Not with me, she doesn't. I'm history. See you around, babe."

Not if I see you first.

The patrolman's glare followed Ramon's retreat to the lounge.

Mallory waited until Mr. Dial-A-Date was out of earshot before she spoke. "Actually, Ramon's the least of my worries. My date went to wash his hands half an hour ago and he's still not back. I'm afraid something may have happened to him."

The patrolman frowned. "That does sound suspicious. Want me to check it out?"

Mallory followed the officer to the men's rest room, but waited outside by the pay phones, where a teenage girl was chattering away, her end of the conversation punctuated by giggles and sweeping hand gestures.

"And then I go, like, you're kidding, right? So he goes, no way! And I go, so prove it. And like, he did." She giggled and smacked her denim-clad thigh. "Is that a scream or what?"

The patrolman reappeared. "Empty. I checked every stall."

"Then where . . ."

"Looks like he took a hike." He shrugged. "It happens."

Jeez. Did she look like the kind of woman who got dumped at Denny's? How pathetic.

"Look, Officer—" she started.

"Lady, I noticed the two of you when you came in. Hate to break it to you, but I've seen punks like that before. Take my word for it, they're nothing but trouble."

"But—"

"Call a cab, go home, and thank your lucky stars all

he stuck you with was the bill." He shrugged again and headed back to his stool at the counter.

"No, for real, Sierra," the girl on the phone squealed. "I am *not* making this up. *Extreme* southern exposure. Right there in the Kmart video department with like a million shoppers doing the blue-light-special thing."

"Damn!" Mallory swore in frustration.

"Problem?" The girl looked up from the phone.

"You might say so. I lost my date."

"Bummer. Just a minute, Sierra." She covered the mouthpiece of the receiver. "Your date. What's he look like?"

"Tall, dark, long hair in a ponytail."

The girl gave her an appraising look. "Oh, yeah. I remember him. The hunk. He went thataway." She hooked a thumb to indicate the exit.

Mallory was halfway through the back door when the girl said something else that brought her to a screeching halt. "What?" She whipped around.

"I said, watch out for the other guy. He wasn't as cute as your hunk."

"The other guy?"

"The one who followed the hunk out the door. The big one."

"Big? How big?"

"Smaller than an elephant . . ." She grinned. "but not by much."

Brody came to with the mother of all headaches. The stink of rotting food—God, he hoped it was food—was all around him. In his nose. In his lungs. In his pores.

But the worst part, the scariest part, was being blind. The darkness was complete. Eyes open or eyes shut made no difference.

He sat up or tried to. His head slammed into solid steel with a resounding clang and he damn near lost consciousness again.

Where the hell was he anyway? And how had he gotten here in the first place? Oh, hell. It hurt to think. It hurt period.

The last thing he remembered was Mallory. He and Mallory were side by side and heading for the car. He could feel her warmth and softness even through all the layers of clothes. He could smell the scent of her perfume and he could hear her voice, low and urgent, saying . . .

"Brody? Are you out here, Brody?"

That wasn't what she'd said. No, it had been something like, "That's odd." And then they'd gone chasing across the street to check out the lights at her neighbor's house.

"Brody, dammit! Where are you?"

Buried alive. That's where he was. Buried alive in a cold, smelly grave. The sickening blend of odors made his stomach roll. Sour milk, rotting fruit, putrefying meat. Oh, hell. He was going to throw up. He gagged, fought down the nausea, groaned, then gagged again.

"Brody? Is that you?" Mallory pounded the side of the big blue Dumpster, her efforts rewarded by another moan. She swore under her breath. Dammit, he was in there and hurt, too, from the sound of it. She grabbed the lid and shoved, but the Dumpster cover didn't budge. Something was holding it down.

"Don't worry, Brody. I'll get you out of there. Just hold on." She dashed back inside the restaurant, where she enlisted the help of the patrolman.

"Here's your problem," he said, when the two of them got outside. "Somebody slapped a couple of these on top."

"What?"

"Sandbags."

"Sandbags? Where would they find sandbags this time of night?"

With a grunt he heaved a second bag onto the pavement at the base of the Dumpster. "Lots of people haul 'em around during the winter months to weigh down the back ends of their pickups. Helps with traction on bad roads."

"But it's April."

The officer shrugged. "So somebody was too lazy or too forgetful to take them out earlier." He shoved the Dumpster cover up and the stench slammed them in the face.

Mallory huffed out a breath, breathing through her mouth. The smell was—in one of her father's favorite colloquialisms—rank enough to gag a maggot off a gut wagon. She stood on tiptoe to peer inside.

The patrolman shone his flashlight on the Dumpster's contents. He uttered a sharp expletive at his first glimpse of the body. Brody's body.

Mallory didn't say a word. Shock flattened her like a sledgehammer blow. Her legs gave way and she slid down the side of the Dumpster to land in a heap on the ground.

Blood. So much blood. Half of Brody's face was obscured by it, sticky with it. He was dead. He must be. No one could survive such a massive blood loss.

Sharp stones cut into her knees. The icy wind raised goose bumps on her flesh. The smell of decay clogged her nose. But she was scarcely aware of her discomfort. Even with her eyes squeezed shut, the blood was all she could see. She wanted to scream or cry, but didn't have the strength for either. Instead she slumped against the Dumpster, concentrating on breathing in and out. On staying alive.

"He's breathing!" The patrolman's sharp cry cut through the layers of shock. "Hey, lady! He's breathing!"

"What kind of rinky-dink hospital is this anyway? I can't believe they didn't keep you overnight for observation." Mallory frowned at Brody as he folded himself into the Jeep's passenger seat.

"Not much night left," he said. The first pale fingers of light poked up above the mountains on the eastern horizon.

"Hmmph." She slammed the door shut hard enough to make him wince, then marched around and got in on the driver's side. She slammed her door, too, and he winced again. "Where to?"

"My place." He was dead tired, in dire need of sleep, but first he'd take a shower. They'd cleaned his head at the hospital, but the rest of him still stank to high heaven. He suspected his queasiness was as much a result of the disgusting odor as the blow to his head.

Mallory turned the key in the ignition and revved the engine. "Which way? I don't know where you live."

Why was she so cranky? She wasn't the one nursing a lump the size of a golf ball.

"The new subdivision off Madison Boulevard, Pilt-down Terrace."

"Fitting address for a Neanderthal," he thought she grumbled, though he couldn't be sure. It was hard to hear over the squeal of the tires and the grinding of the gears.

"Okay, what's the problem, Mallory?"

"I don't have a problem. You're the one with the problem." She took the right onto Ninth Avenue on two wheels. He'd swear she was hitting every pothole on purpose.

Brody grabbed his head. All he needed was a good case of whiplash on top of everything else. "You're right. I do have a problem. I'm trapped in a car with a maniac driver. Slow it down, okay?"

Mallory tucked the corners of her mouth in tight and shot him a look that would have wilted a lesser man, but she did slow down to thirty. "What did you think you were doing investigating that truck without backup? Without even telling me where you were going?"

"Couldn't see any point in worrying you."

"Worrying me? *Worrying* me? I sat inside the restaurant stewing for half an hour. If I'd known you'd gone out to the parking lot to play Sam Spade, I would have checked on you sooner. Dammit, half an hour! You could have bled to death, Brody Hunter!"

"Bled to death? The blow didn't even break the skin."

"Well, I didn't know that. I looked in that Dumpster and darned near had a stroke."

"It was only spaghetti sauce, Mallory."

"Well, it looked like blood, dammit!" She jerked the Jeep to the side of the road and killed the engine. Her hands were shaking. She looked sick.

"Mallory." Brody laid his hand on hers. "I'm sorry."

She took a long, quivering breath, then turned to face him. "No, I'm the one who's sorry. I'm acting like an idiot. But dammit, Brody, you scared me."

He gave her hand a squeeze. "Scared me too."

Mallory woke a little before noon. She was stiff from trying to sleep curled up in a chair. Brody, on the other hand, was sleeping like a baby. He lay diagonally across bed, rolled up in the covers like a human enchilada.

How would it feel to be tucked in there with him, to have his big, warm body spooned along her backside, his arms wrapped around her, holding her close? How would it feel to have his breath tickling her neck? His . . . Oh, boy.

Mallory's heart raced; her cheeks grew warm. Jeez, what was the matter with her? If Brody woke up and saw her slobbering all over him like some sex-starved old maid, she'd probably give *him* a stroke. Or at the very least, the wrong idea.

Who are you kidding, Scott? You're the one with all the wrong ideas. You're the one whose hormones have run amok. You're the one whose body is tingling in anticipation.

The problem was she could be one big tingle from head to toe and it still wouldn't make any difference. Sooner or later the memories would kick in and short out her libido.

She threw off the blanket covering her and stood up, shivering in the borrowed T-shirt and sweatpants she'd donned after her shower. Her chic new dress lay crumpled in a heap next to the chair. Eighty bucks down the drain.

Terrified that Brody's injuries were life threatening, she'd cradled his head in her lap all the way to the emergency room. She'd been relieved to learn he wasn't dying after all, but by that time the dress was a goner, permanently stained with spaghetti sauce.

Mallory checked her watch. Noon. The emergency-room doctor had given her strict instructions to wake Brody every couple hours or so to make certain he didn't slip into a coma. She'd roused him last a little over three hours ago, shortly before she'd zonked out herself. She really ought to wake him again, but he looked so comfortable, she hated to disturb him.

Yeah, but what if he wasn't sleeping? What if he'd already lapsed into a coma?

She nudged his shoulder. He snorted once and rolled over onto his back. Did people in comas move around like that?

Brody Hunter lay spread-eagled across the king-sized bed, snoring like a chain saw. She frowned at him. No man had a right to be so damn gorgeous, particularly when he wasn't even trying.

His thick, black hair spread out on the pillows in tangled disarray. A loose tendril curled against one lean cheek. She longed to brush it away but didn't dare. She'd die of embarrassment if he caught her taking such a liberty.

Even with a double layer of lash-building mascara,

her eyelashes were no match for his. Long and lush, they
fanned out against his cheeks, the only hint of softness in
an angular face.

One brown arm was flung out to the side, the other
bent at the elbow, his hand resting on his chest. A big,
blunt hand she suspected was capable of handling a gun
or a woman with equal finesse. Mallory shivered.

Enough of that, girl.

She gave his shoulder a shake. "Wake up, Brody."

He groaned and thrashed around, flinging half his
covers aside to expose one muscular brown leg to the
thigh. Then he settled back into the mattress with a sigh
and started snoring again.

He didn't want to wake up, and Mallory didn't know
whether to be worried or not. Not waking up was bad,
but people in comas didn't snore, did they? Or did they?
Dammit, she was a teacher, not a nurse. What was she
supposed to do now?

If at first you don't succeed . . .

She prodded his shoulder again, harder this time.
"Wake up, Brody!"

He gave one last grunting snort and opened his eyes.
He blinked several times, frowning as if his head ached.
Then he caught sight of her, and a smile spread across
his face.

"What?" Mallory did her best to appear nonchalant.
Surely he hadn't been faking the snores. Surely he hadn't
seen her practically drooling over him.

"You're nice to wake up to, that's all. Almost makes
up for the jackhammers in my head. What'd you do?
Get me drunk so you could take advantage of me?"

"Don't you remember?"

He frowned. "Oh, yeah. The Dumpster."

"Followed by a visit to Brunswick General and a second interview with the cops. Not the sort of date I'm used to."

He grinned. "At least it wasn't boring." He reached out and captured her hand between his. "Bet you never slept over on the first date before."

"I didn't exactly. . . ." Mallory stared down at their clasped hands. Brody twined the fingers of one hand through hers while he used the other to trace the tendons on the back of her hand. If pinching her earlobe had been tingle to the tenth power, this was tingle to the hundredth. Her heart did an Olympic-caliber double axel. Oh, boy.

"I want to thank you for saving my life."

"But I didn't. Your situation was never really life threatening." She couldn't meet his gaze.

"What do you call damned near gagging to death?" Brody fell silent for a moment, then said, "Mallory, look at me."

She did and her racing heart skipped a beat at the tender expression on his face.

"Thanks. Thanks for everything." He tugged gently on her hand, pulling her down on the edge of the bed.

He was going to kiss her. She could tell by the look in his eyes. And she was going to let him. The look in his eyes told her that too. Her heartbeat thundered in her ears, so loud she almost missed hearing his beeper go off.

But Brody heard it. The smoky heat in his eyes vanished in the space of a heartbeat. "Damn," he said. He closed his eyes for a second and she saw regret flicker across his face. When he opened his eyes again, they held the glitter of steel. He dropped her hand. "Where's my pager?"

She dug it from the pocket of his discarded jacket and passed it to him along with the phone.

While he called in, Mallory wandered out to the high-ceilinged living room and glanced out one of the big front windows. She took a startled step back when she saw the black Lexus parked across the street. Jeez, surely Lindsey and Evan hadn't tracked her here! Her heart raced again, but this time it wasn't passion that triggered the response.

She took a series of deep breaths. Okay, it was a black Lexus, but Evan Corby didn't own the only black Lexus in town.

Or did he? Her heart sank as she saw Evan's familiar form emerge from the house directly across the street. It plummeted clear to her socks when she saw the gorgeous brunette waving to him from the recessed doorway. What was he up to?

Evan paused at the curb next to his car, looking up and down the street as if he were taking inventory. His gaze seemed to linger on Brody's house, and for a split second Mallory feared he'd spotted her. But he hadn't. He couldn't have. Otherwise he wouldn't have climbed into the driver's seat and driven away without a backward glance.

Oh, boy. She backed away from the window until she bumped into a chair. She sat, trying to make some sense of her swirling thoughts. This was terrible. This was worse than terrible. In six days Evan was supposed to marry her sister. So what was he doing at the brunette's house?

There was probably a simple explanation, an innocent explanation, but she was darned if she could think what it might be. The buxom brunette had looked vaguely familiar, though Mallory couldn't quite place her. One thing for certain, she wasn't the bride-to-be.

Maybe Lindsey's suspicions had some basis in fact. Like it or not, maybe Mallory really should have a little chat with Evan.

FIVE

Brody found Mallory in the living room staring at the dusty split-leaf philodendron in the corner as if she'd never seen one before. "Problem?" he asked.

"What?" She turned slowly to face him. "Oh, no. It's nothing. Who was on the phone?"

"Lieutenant Kirkwood."

"On a Sunday? I thought officers were strictly nine-to-fivers."

"None of us will be nine-to-fivers again until we catch the burglars." And GI Joe. The rapist had attacked another victim last night, according to Kirkwood.

"Were they able to trace the pickup, using the partial you gave them?"

"Yeah, only one truck registered in Paiute County fit the description, so they hauled the owner in for questioning. The lieutenant wants us to come down to see if we can ID the guy."

"But what about your head? Didn't you tell him you were on the casualty list?"

He'd slept well and the golf-ball-sized lump on the back of his head had shrunk to mosquito-bite proportions. Aside from a headache, he felt pretty good. "I'm okay. How about you?"

Mallory looked pale and fragile with her hair wisping around her face and faint violet shadows under her eyes. Then she grinned at him and the illusion of fragility vanished. "I'll live. Did your lieutenant say who the owner of the truck was?"

"Arlo Davis. Name ring a bell?"

She shook her head. "Never heard of him, but I bet it's the same guy we saw outside Dixon and Alexandra Yano's house. And probably the same one who clobbered you, then stashed you in the Dumpster. According to the witness, the man who followed you outside was 'smaller than an elephant, but not by much.' "

Brody nodded. "Good description of our burglary suspect, all right."

Unfortunately, the witness's description wasn't a good match for Arlo Davis, a frail, white-haired man in his late seventies.

"I don't get it," said Mallory. "Why did they just let him go? Even if he wasn't the human tank who bashed you over the head and ripped off my friends' house, the old boy had to have some idea who the culprit was. After all, we know it was his truck that was used in the robbery."

"No," said Brody. "We don't know it was his truck. All we know is that it was a truck that looked like his. I didn't get the partial license number at the crime scene."

"Yes, but someone attacked you when you bent down

to check the plate number on Davis's truck. That can't be a coincidence."

He shrugged. "No, but it's not evidence, either. Maybe if Arlo Davis had been the big guy we saw at the Yano house, we could have convinced a judge to issue a search warrant so we could have checked his truck and his house for stolen goods. As it is, we've got nothing except, in my case, a killer of a headache. I'm going back to bed to take it easy like the doctor said, but . . ." A smile spread slowly across his face.

Mallory felt the reaction all the way to her toes. "But what?"

"Why don't we try this dinner-date thing one more time? Say tomorrow night at seven?"

She frowned. "I don't know, Brody. I think the fates are trying to tell us something." Another date wasn't a good idea. She was way too attracted to him already, and she suspected he wasn't exactly indifferent to her. Normally a strong mutual attraction was a good thing, but Mallory's approach to relationships wasn't normal. Her fear of intimacy ran deep. She and Brody had no future, and it wasn't fair to him to pretend otherwise. All she needed was an escort for the wedding festivities. Nothing more.

"Come on, Mallory. Give me a chance to make it up to you."

She gave an involuntary shiver of excitement at the look in his eyes. "No. I'm not really your type, Brody. We have nothing in common."

"What are you talking about? I love hot-fudge sundaes and you love hot-fudge sundaes. I love puppies and sunsets and long walks on the beach. And you—"

"Love kittens and sunrises and curling up in a chair with a good book. I rest my case."

"Hell, woman, give me a chance. We spent the night together, and you survived that. This time I'm only asking you out to dinner."

"Last time you only asked me out to dinner."

Brody laughed. "So I did, but I plead extenuating circumstances. Please, Mallory. It'll be my way of thanking you for all you did last night."

The look of entreaty on his handsome face was hard to resist.

She bit down on her lower lip. "No, I don't think so." Jeez, why did he have to smile like that? Her pulse pounded in her ears like heavy surf. She felt a little dizzy and a lot shaky. But she could hold out as long as he didn't touch her.

He touched her, a double whammy, one hand on her arm, the other cupping her chin. Electroshock therapy couldn't deliver any more voltage than the gentle pressure of his fingertips. "Please, Mallory?"

Hard to resist? Ha! Make that darned near impossible to resist.

"Mallory?" A whisper of sound that shuddered down her spine. She shivered in anticipation.

He leaned closer, brushing her lips with his. "Please?" he asked, his mouth so close to hers, she felt the words as well as heard them.

Oh, boy. She closed her eyes to shut out the sweet intensity of his expression, but it didn't help.

He kissed her eyelids and she went limp in reaction. His hand on her arm was all that kept her upright. "Please, Mallory. Say yes."

She took a deep breath, fully intending to tell him no. "Yes," she said instead, and he hugged her tight.

"Good girl."

No, dumb girl. Stupid girl. Idiot girl. "What time did you say?" Her voice emerged as a choked whisper.

"Seven."

She opened her eyes to find him smiling down at her. "I'll be ready."

"And I'll be there."

Yeah, sure he would. By seven-thirty or a quarter to eight. She was learning.

Brody dropped Mallory at her house at a little after three. She planned to catch up on some laundry, run over to Aerobics Plus for an hour or so to work some of the kinks out of her muscles, then coddle herself with a bubble bath.

Her sister screwed up the schedule.

"Where have you been?" Lindsey launched her attack before Mallory was through the door.

"Out." She glanced pointedly at the empty soda can on the end table, the rumpled *TV Guide*, the blaring television. "You certainly know how to make yourself at home."

The sarcasm was wasted on Lindsey. She frowned. "You didn't come home last night. I waited up for you until after midnight. This morning I started calling at five, then punched redial again every fifteen minutes until Evan dropped me off about ten. What have you been doing all this time?"

"Long version or short version?"

"How about the PG version?"

"With me, every version's a PG version."

"That Brody Hunter's X-rated if I ever saw X-rated."

"He just looks X-rated. He's really very sweet."

Lindsey shot her a skeptical look.

"Okay, don't believe me, then. Here's the short version, editing out all the sex orgies and most of the violence."

Lindsey rolled her eyes.

"First, I interrupted a burglary and consequently spent hours wading through a sea of red tape down at police headquarters. Then—"

"Mother said you'd called."

"Right, so then Brody took me to Denny's—we'd missed dinner and both of us were starving—and that's where I discovered what I thought was a dead body in the Dumpster."

"Wait! Why were you pawing through a Dumpster at Denny's?"

"I was looking for Brody. He left to go wash his hands and never came back."

"Oh, sure, that explains it. Dumpster'd be the first place I'd check for a missing boyfriend." Lindsey made a face. "So who was the body in the Dumpster?"

"Brody, of course. He wasn't really dead, though."

Lindsey nodded. "Yeah, I kinda figured that since I just saw him drop you off."

Mallory knew she wasn't making much sense; she was too tired to think clearly, let alone frame coherent sentences. She hung her coat and shoulder bag on the hall tree, kicked her shoes off, and collapsed on a chair, yawning so widely she felt as if her jaw were about to come unhinged.

"What happened? Did he pick a bar brawl with the wrong guy?"

"Lindsey, just let it drop. I didn't get a whole lot of sleep and I'm not in the mood for a cross-examination."

"Didn't get a whole lot of sleep? You mean . . . How long have you known this man, Mal?"

"Long enough."

"You should be careful. Evan and I discussed Brody Hunter and we both decided he's bad news. As an investigative reporter, Evan's seen guys like that before—usually in handcuffs. Evan said he wouldn't be surprised to discover Brody Hunter was on the FBI's most wanted list. He has the kind of face you find decorating the post-office wall."

"Brody's a cop, not a crook. I think Evan's been watching too much tabloid TV."

"Hunter claims to be a cop, but how do you know he really is? Have you checked him out with the department?"

"Linz, believe me, he's legit. If you need references, though, check with Kyle Brewster. They went to school together."

"That was years ago. A lot could have happened since then."

"Just drop it, Lindsey. He's a cop. Period."

"Or is he a cop, question mark?"

"Meaning?"

"Meaning not all police officers are patterns of virtue. Brody Hunter could still be—as Daddy would say—crooked as a dog's hind leg. Just study the man objectively, Mal, and tell me he doesn't look like the type who might be into something really scary, like drugs or illegal arms deals."

"Right. Or maybe he's a hit man or a serial killer or an international terrorist, wanted on six continents."

"You think it's a joke, don't you?" Lindsey fiddled with the piping that edged one of the throw pillows piled at the end of the sofa. A frown etched a pair of creases between her eyebrows.

Guilt niggled at Mallory's conscience. Lindsey was worried about her, and flippancy was a pretty poor return for her concern. "Look, I'm sorry we missed the dinner last night, but it truly was unavoidable."

Lindsey waved away her apology. "Yes, I know. Mother explained all that." Lindsey tossed the pillow aside. "Mallory, you just don't get it. I'm worried about you."

"Why? I'm fine."

"You're not fine. You're acting completely out of character. Missing a dinner engagement. Staying out all night. Evan says . . ."

"Evan says what?" Mallory snapped.

Lindsey's chin came up sharply. "Evan says you're upset about the two of us getting married."

Mallory was so surprised, she couldn't utter a word.

Lindsey stared hard at her. "Are you upset? I know you dated Evan for years, but it wasn't like you were engaged or anything. Or even had much of a relationship."

"What do you mean?"

"You don't have to pretend, Mallory. Evan told me about your problem."

"How very indiscreet of him." Mallory forced a laugh. "But then, he always did talk too much." She cleared her throat. She wasn't going to cry, dammit. She hadn't cried in years and she wasn't about to start now.

"Tell Evan to stop worrying. I'm not upset or jealous or angry or hurt. When I first heard the news, I admit I was . . . surprised. At first. But I got over it." She smiled grimly. "So everybody can just stop worrying about Mallory, okay?"

Lindsey's gaze probed Mallory's for a long, silent moment. "You're sure?"

"I'm positive." She paused. "Anything else I can help you with?"

Lindsey clenched her fists. "Evan's still acting weird."

So she'd noticed. Mallory struggled to arrange her expression into one of caring concern combined with a hint of detachment. "What's he up to now?" As if she didn't know.

"This morning Evan said he had some business to take care of, but he wouldn't tell me what it was and he refused to let me go with him."

I should tell her what I saw. "Maybe he didn't want you to be bored."

"Oh, give me a break, Mal. He just didn't want me to know what he was up to. Who schedules business meetings on Sunday morning anyway?"

"Maybe he had to catch the minister before church." *I really ought to tell her.*

"Minister schminister. The only business he was up to was monkey business!" Lindsey was working herself up to another tantrum.

Forget it. My lips are sealed. If she starts crying now, I won't get rid of her for hours.

"What makes you so sure Evan's seeing someone else?"

"I'm not sure," Lindsey said, "but I'm damned suspicious."

"Why? Because he got a few phone calls? Because he didn't want you with him this morning?"

"That, yes. But . . ." She choked on a sob.

Oh, boy. Here we go.

Lindsey took a deep breath and pulled herself together. "Yesterday we stopped at the mall to pick up some ribbons and silk flowers Mother had ordered to trim the gazebo and we saw a woman in the parking lot. She practically ran her car into a light pole she was so busy trying to catch Evan's attention, but he pretended not to see her."

"So maybe she was one of his fans. And maybe he was in too big a hurry to bother with an autograph."

"Oh, please. Evan's never too busy to give out autographs. He thrives on attention. You know that. No, he just didn't want to have to introduce me to her. That's why he pretended not to notice her. Good grief. A man would have to be blind not to notice a voluptuous brunette like that, especially one dressed in a low-necked leotard."

Voluptuous brunette. Leotard. Suddenly it all clicked and Mallory realized why the woman she'd seen with Evan earlier had looked vaguely familiar. Lamour Hooterman. Her husband, George "Hootie" Hooterman, a former navy SEAL, owned and operated Aerobics Plus where Mallory worked out. Jealous to the nth degree, Hootie'd been known to blacken a man's eyes just for winking at Lamour.

What was wrong with Evan? Did he have a death wish?

❖———————————❖

"You're not dressed," said Brody, though in point of fact she *was* dressed—in her old blue sweats and an Eastern Oregon University T-shirt. "I said seven. Didn't I say seven?"

Mallory smiled at his confusion. "Yes, but it's only ten after. I wasn't expecting you for another twenty minutes at least. Come on in. It won't take me but a second to change. Where are we going anyway?" Somewhere dressy by the looks of him. He wore black slacks and a matching sport coat over a white turtleneck, and she had to admit Lindsey was right. He did look like a criminal, the Hollywood version of a Mafia hit man. But drop-dead gorgeous all the same.

He glanced at his watch. "We have seven-thirty reservations at Zachary's on the River."

"Wow. Obviously police detectives make more than fifth-grade teachers."

"Or maybe they just spend more when they're trying to impress someone."

Mallory's teasing smile wobbled at the edges, then collapsed altogether. Impress someone? Like her? Oh, boy. This was not good. Not, not, not. "Uh, Brody, I—"

"Hurry up, Mallory. It's late."

Not too late, she hoped.

"Dinner was divine," Mallory told Brody as he helped her into the passenger's seat of his Jeep. Which, come to think of it, was pretty strange since *divine* wasn't a word she bandied about too often. They'd had wine with their meal. Maybe that explained it.

Brody scraped a bow, then struck a jaunty pose beside the open door. "Where to now, milady?"

Mallory's gurgle of laughter came perilously close to a giggle. Definitely the wine. "Milady, is it? How very eighteenth century."

A wicked grin tilted Brody's mouth. "Well, hell. It sounds a little classier than 'Your place or mine?'—don't you think?"

"It does," she agreed, wondering why the warning bells weren't going off. They should be ringing like crazy by now. She knew what that grin meant. Danger with a capital *D*. Trouble with a capital *T*.

"So?" He shrugged. "Which is it? Your place or mine?"

"Neither," she said. "It's only a little after nine. I'm not ready to go home yet."

He lifted an eyebrow. "You mean you're not ready to go home with me yet."

"No, I . . . that is yes, but . . ." She stammered to a halt as he dropped a kiss on the end of her nose.

"Don't look so worried, honey. I can handle rejection."

Brody shut her door and circled around to the driver's side, where he slid himself under the wheel. The engine caught with a roar and he pulled onto the road.

Mallory studied him in the light from the dash. Brody had a terrific profile: straight nose, firm jaw, great cheekbones, eyelashes any woman would kill to possess. And she loved the way the short hairs, the ones that weren't long enough for the ponytail, curled softly, hugging the back of his neck all along his hairline, a little imperfection, a hint of vulnerability in an otherwise perfect tough-guy facade.

What she liked best about Brody Hunter, though, wasn't his looks, but the fact that he was just as nice to be with as he was to look at. She sighed. "We need to talk."

Brody cowered away in mock fear. "Oh, no. Isn't that what the girl always says right before she tells the guy to take a hike? Hey, forget everything I said before. The truth is, I'm lousy at rejection."

Mallory bit her lip. He wasn't making this any easier. "Brody, there are things about me you don't know."

"Just as there are things about me you don't know, honey. Learning to know another human being isn't as simple as memorizing a nursery rhyme."

"No, it's more like memorizing an entire set of encyclopedias."

"Right. People are complex creatures and building a solid friendship takes time."

"Friendship? Is that what we're building?"

"Absolutely. A very special friendship."

Which was good news, right? So why did she feel like she'd just taken a shot to the solar plexus? "Friendship," she muttered to herself.

"And speaking of friends," said Brody, "I just remembered. Kyle asked if we'd stop by after dinner. He said he has something for you."

"What kind of something?" It wasn't Christmas and her birthday wasn't for another month. What was Kyle up to?

"He made me promise not to tell."

Kyle lived in a quiet cul-de-sac in one of the older sections of town. His house was a three-story Victorian painted mauve and burgundy with white gingerbread trim. The house had been a decrepit wreck when Kyle bought it three years earlier, but he was slowly returning it to its former glory.

A '65 Mustang, lemon yellow in the glow of the streetlights, was parked on the gravel in front of the carriage house. Brody pulled up next to it.

"Nice," he said. "I didn't know Kyle was a car enthusiast."

"He's not," Mallory said. "He drives a six-year-old Taurus. Gunmetal gray with a pale gray interior and a Triple A sticker in the window. He must have company."

They rang the bell, and Tim, the bartender from the Blue Russian, opened the door, answering her question about the car's ownership. "Ooh, don't we look nice?" he murmured as he ushered them into the foyer.

"Where's Kyle?" Mallory asked. Tim seemed to be right at home. He'd evidently just gotten off work. He was still wearing the tight black pants and flowing white shirt of his Blue Russian uniform, though he'd dispensed with the short, tasseled vest.

He gestured vaguely. "Kyle's grubbing away in the bowels of the house. I'd take you back, but I was just on my way out. I tried to convince him to come out for a drink, but he'd rather play handyman." His charm and his pout were both wasted on Mallory. In her opinion, the man was almost as big a fake as Ramon from Dial-A-Date.

She and Brody found Kyle in the butler's pantry, stripping layers of old paint from the woodwork.

He looked up from the baseboard and let out a low whistle of approval. "Nice outfit, Mallory," he said in reference to her fitted peach-colored silk jacket and matching slacks. "Is that mascara I see on your lashes? Blusher on your cheeks?"

"Brody took me to Zachary's. They frown on sweats and sneakers." And the makeup was an experiment, she told herself. She was practicing for the wedding. Her sudden interest in eyeliner and lipstick had nothing to do with wanting to look attractive for Brody Hunter. Not a thing.

Kyle raised an eyebrow. "Did you try the trout?"

"No," Brody said. "Filet mignon."

Kyle lifted his other eyebrow. "My, my, my."

Mallory frowned. "There's no 'my, my, my' about it. Dinner was my reward for pulling him out of the Dumpster at Denny's Saturday night. Did you hear about that?"

"I did indeed." Kyle shoved himself to his feet, setting aside his paintbrush and the can of smelly chemical stripper. "Which is why I asked Brody to bring you by tonight."

He scrubbed his hands at the chipped porcelain sink and dried them on a towel that hung from a rickety wall rack. "As I wandered through the mall on my lunch hour today, I saw something that reminded me of you, Mallory." He led the way to the spacious formal dining room. "You haven't seen the new wallpaper in here yet, have you? What do you think?"

It was gorgeous, a rich floral design in rose and teal on a cream background. "I love it!"

Kyle glowed with pleasure at her enthusiastic response. "Yes, and I ordered coordinating fabric for the valance and chair cushions. With a narrow teal piping, I thought. Or maybe the rose?"

"Teal. Definitely teal," Mallory said.

"What do you think, Brody?" Kyle held up sample swatches.

"The green or the pink? Either one would look good on Mallory."

"On me?" Mallory laughed. "Kyle was talking about drapes."

"Drapes?" Brody looked confused. "You bought her drapes? I thought you got her a dress."

Kyle frowned in pretended irritation. "I did. And you've spoiled the surprise, thank you very much." He picked up a box from the sideboard and passed it to Mallory. "For you. To make up for the one that was ruined."

"Kyle, you didn't have to . . . oh!" She stopped, speechless with delight as she saw what lay folded inside on a bed of tissue. "The blue dress." The one she hadn't been able to afford. "Kyle, you shouldn't have."

"You need a dress for the rehearsal dinner."

"But it's so expensive!"

Brody stroked the soft fabric with his fingertips. "It matches your eyes," he said. She glanced up quickly. The expression on his face set her blood pounding thickly through her veins. She watched his big brown hand stroke the fabric again and felt as if he were stroking her. His hand was broad, with heavy knuckles and a light dusting of black hair, yet his fingers moved across the silky material with a gentle touch. A lover's touch. Her nipples tightened, and she shivered despite the fact that she was experiencing her own little tropical heat wave.

"Call it an early birthday present," Kyle suggested.

"What?" Mallory was having trouble staying focused on the conversation. "Oh, the dress. Right. It's beautiful, but you shouldn't have."

Kyle looked from her to Brody, then back again. His

lips twitched. "Think of me as your fairy godfather," he said. His eyes twinkled.

Brody walked Mallory to her door. She clutched the big dress box to her chest as if it were a shield and he were a dragon.

"Mallory?"

"Hmm?" Her glasses had slipped down to the end of her nose and he nudged them back up where they belonged. Her eyes grew large and her lips parted on a nearly inaudible sigh.

Brody slipped the box from her unresisting hands, set it down on the deck, and leaned in closer to kiss her good night. Just a peck was all he intended to give her, but the taste of her mouth under his, the smell of her perfume, the feel of her body soft and warm and close to his all combined to change his mind. What started as a sweet little peck became something altogether more dangerous.

Mallory was fun, sweet, and intelligent. He enjoyed her company and valued their growing friendship, but in that instant Brody realized he didn't just like her, he wanted her too.

The question was, did she want him? Sometimes he thought the answer was yes. Yesterday, for example, he'd caught a fleeting expression on her face when she stood by his bed. And tonight at Kyle's, he'd surprised that look again. It was an expression he'd be hard put to describe. Not lust. Nothing so crude. More like awareness. Or an awakening sensuality.

But other times, too many other times, she looked at him as if she were afraid of him.

Not now, though. Now she was softness and warmth and the sweet seduction of this endless kiss.

He backed her into the door, one hand cradling the nape of her neck. Slanting his mouth across hers, he deepened the kiss while he slid his other hand up under her coat to cup her breast.

She stiffened and jerked away with a strangled cry. The next thing he knew he was flat on his back, sucking air and wondering what the hell just happened.

SIX

"Sorry," Mallory said, embarrassment clogging her throat. "Are you okay?" Dammit, she'd overreacted again. Just like she always did.

Propping himself on his elbows, Brody shot her an owlish look. "What was that? Karate? Kung fu?"

"Basic self-defense, a little move I learned from Hootie, my aerobics instructor." She smiled apologetically. "Sorry," she repeated.

"No, it was my fault." He stood up and brushed himself off. "Apparently I pressed the wrong buttons."

"Something like that." Mortified, she couldn't bring herself to look at him.

He touched her lightly on the shoulder. "Want to talk about it?"

"What? My career as the body-slamming self-defense queen of Brunswick?" Her attempt at laughter sounded pretty sick.

"No." He tilted her chin up so their gazes met. "The reason you learned to defend yourself in the first place."

His eyes were soft and understanding. Mallory felt her own fill with tears.

She jerked away so he wouldn't see, and he took a step back. *Probably thinks I'm going to dump him again.* "I don't want to talk about it."

"Maybe you should, though. What happened, Mallory?"

"Happened?" Startled, she flicked her gaze back up to his. "What makes you think anything happened?"

His gaze held hers. "Am I wrong?"

"Let's just say I have a problem and leave it at that."

He brushed a tear from her cheek. "And what if I don't want to leave it at that?"

The quick anger, never far from the surface, spurted up. He thought he understood her. But he was wrong.

Dammit, she didn't want his insight or his pity, either. She flailed out to shove him away, but he caught her hand and tucked it between his.

"Let go!"

"Not until you talk to me."

"Don't you get it, Hunter? This topic is not open for discussion. I can't talk about it. I *won't* talk about it."

"Fine. Just listen then. Remember I told you that you reminded me of someone?"

She nodded.

A muscle twitched near the corner of his mouth. "Well, that someone was my sister, Jenna."

"Was?" Her heart skipped a beat and her anger seeped away.

"She drove her car off a cliff two weeks before she was supposed to graduate from high school."

"I'm sorry."

"Jenna didn't talk to anyone, either, but six months

after she died I found a password-protected file on her computer that held all her secrets." He stared across the street toward the Yano house.

"What secrets?" she asked.

"Jenna'd been dating a man named Ryan Lucas on the sly. Lucas had a rotten—and well-deserved—reputation. Jenna knew I hated the sonuvabitch, but convinced herself it was because I didn't 'understand' him. After all, with his dad in prison and his mother dead, he was bound to have a few rough edges. Rough edges . . ." Brody's voice was hoarse with suppressed emotion.

"On their second date he drove out to the boonies and put the moves on her," he continued. "She said stop. He didn't."

"Date rape," Mallory whispered.

"Yeah, only Lucas convinced Jenna it was her fault, said she'd pushed him past the point of no return. Hell, she didn't have any experience, didn't know any better than to believe him.

"She didn't tell a soul, not then and not two months later when she found out she was pregnant. When Lucas learned he was about to become a daddy, he skipped town . . . and Jenna took a shortcut to eternity."

Pain knotted in her chest. "I don't know what to say."

Brody squeezed her hand tightly. "I couldn't help Jenna, but maybe I can help you."

"Brody . . ." She shook her head. "I know you mean well, but I can't talk about this." Her voice shook. "Please understand."

He released her hand, stooped to retrieve the dress box, and handed it to her. "If you change your mind, I'll be around." One corner of his mouth quirked up in a crooked little half smile that put a knot in her chest and a lump in her throat.

Brody didn't talk to Mallory for the next three days, but she was never far from his thoughts. On Tuesday he stopped off at the diner for lunch. His heart did a drumroll when he caught sight of her familiar blonde head in the back booth. He made an unnecessary trip to the men's room just so he'd have an excuse to stop and say hi on the way past. He even had the first syllable of her name out before he realized the blonde was a stranger, ten years older than Mallory and fifteen pounds heavier.

By Thursday he was taking his stress out on his co-workers. Regan Armstrong and Cesar Rios gave as good as they got, but Annie Graves, one of the day-shift dispatchers, was another story. He hated like hell to see her cower away every time he got within ten feet of her. Made him feel like a bully.

This is stupid, he told himself. You're acting like a lovesick pup. Call her. You owe it to yourself. Hell, he owed it to everyone at city hall.

But call her and say what? *I really want to take our relationship a step further, so let's get this problem of yours out in the open?* Not hardly. He didn't want to scare her.

So how about, *I think I'm beginning to care for you and it tears me up to see you so unhappy?* Better, though the caring part still might trip her alarm.

No, what he needed was a legitimate reason to get in touch. Or even a phony, trumped-up reason. Like . . . police business.

Sitting at his desk, surrounded by paperwork, Brody smiled for the first time since Monday night.

"You look like something the cat dragged in." April Scott bulldozed her way past Mallory into the living room.

"Hello, Mother. Nice to see you too. I'm fine. A little hungover, but basically all right. Thanks for asking."

"Sarcasm doesn't become you." April made herself at home on one end of the love seat.

Settling in for the interrogation, Mallory thought grimly. Probably has a set of thumbscrews and a portable rack in her purse. "To what do I owe the pleasure?"

"If the mountain won't come to Muhammad . . ." April shrugged. "How are you? We haven't seen much of you lately."

Mallory forced a smile. "I've been busy." Depilling her sweaters. Alphabetizing her spice rack. "I keep meaning to drop by, but time gets away from me." Last night she'd been invited to her parents' house for dinner again. Instead, she'd ended up at Kyle's, drinking wine coolers like they were soda pop and bawling her way through *Thelma and Louise*.

"I called here four times last night. No answer." April's eyebrows drew together in a frown. "What were you doing all evening?"

"Not what you're thinking."

"What I'm thinking is my daughter may be in trouble."

"I'm fine, Mother."

"Fine? Excuse me? By your own admission you're

hungover, and, Mallory, normally you don't even drink. I think your new boyfriend is a bad influence. Lindsey doesn't trust him and neither does Evan."

"Lindsey and Evan don't know what they're talking about."

April lifted an eyebrow. "I understand you spent the night at his house on Saturday."

"Good grief! How many times do I have to go over this? It was perfectly innocent. Brody'd had a bump on the head. I just hung around to make sure he didn't slip into a coma. Fortunately, his injury wasn't as serious as we thought."

April shook her head. "Sounds to me like he's taking advantage of you. How long have you known him?"

"Awhile."

"Oh, very precise," her mother snapped. "Is that awhile seven months or awhile seven hours?"

Closer to seven days, but she wasn't about to let that slip. Mallory shrugged. "Just awhile. I don't know for sure. I gave up keeping a diary when I was eleven."

Her mother had gestapo eyes, ice blue. *Ve haf vays of making you talk.* Mallory shifted her gaze to April's handbag. All right. Reality check here. It was a big sucker, first cousin to a suitcase, but probably not big enough to conceal an iron maiden, though maybe a rubber hose. . . .

"So how did you meet him? Where is he from? Why have you been so secretive about him?" Her mother rattled off questions in her best machine-gun style.

Mallory sat up straight, ticking off the answers on her fingers. "Kyle Brewster introduced us. Brody's from Pendleton, but he lives here now. And I didn't talk about him because I didn't think it was any of your business. I *am* a grown woman, Mother."

April muttered something under her breath.

Mallory hated when she did that. "If you have something to say, spit it out."

Her mother's expression was sour. "I said, you don't act like it."

Silently, Mallory counted to ten. Why couldn't she and her mother have a normal conversation? Their communication seemed to be limited to social chitchat or arguments. Nothing in between. "Perhaps if you treated me like an adult . . ."

"Well, maybe I would if you didn't pout like a spoiled brat. You've had your nose out of joint for the past four months."

"Well, pardon me for being human, Mother. When the guy you've dated for the last eleven years suddenly pops the question to your younger sister, it tends to color your outlook."

"So I noticed. Green with envy." Suddenly April's face softened. She reached for Mallory's hands. "Admit it, Mallory. You were never in love with Evan. He was just a habit."

Mallory frowned. "A bad habit."

"Exactly, because you and Evan were wrong for each other. But Lindsey's in love with him and he's in love with her. You need to let go."

Mallory sighed. "Yes, Mother." *Now go home. You've done the interrogation and delivered your lecture du jour.*

April Scott smiled. "I wouldn't interfere if I weren't worried about you, baby. You wasted eleven years on Evan and now you're hung up on another man who's totally wrong for you."

"I'm not hung up on Brody! Where did you get that idea?" *And what makes you think he's so wrong for me?*

"Well, gee, where did I get that idea?" Her mother stroked her chin and stared off into space. "Maybe it was when you announced your date for the wedding was the studmuffin of the universe."

Mallory cringed. Oh, yeah. She had said something of the kind, but only because Lindsey had been rubbing salt in her wounds for months, going on and on ad nauseam about the wedding.

April tugged at her lip. "Or maybe it was the fact you skipped out on dinner with Uncle Toby and Aunt Chloe only to end up staying out all night doing God knows what."

"I explained that."

"Uh-huh. Or tried to." Her mother's look said she wasn't buying it. "Or maybe it was last night's drunken orgy."

"Drunken orgy? How does a few wine coolers and an R-rated video translate to a drunken orgy? I just—"

"Just?"

"Not that it's any of your business, but I spent the evening with Kyle Brewster."

Her mother looked skeptical. "Kyle? The one who went to school with this outlaw you're sleeping with?"

"Outlaw?" Mallory made a face. "Where do you get this stuff? Brody's a cop, Mother. And for your information, we're not sleeping together. Yet."

April made a strangled sound. "What do you mean 'yet'?" she demanded as the doorbell rang.

"Just a minute." Grateful for the reprieve, Mallory practically ran to the door. She peered through the peephole only to find Brody peering back. Distorted by the lens, he grinned at her, revealing huge teeth in an even huger face. His top-heavy body tapered down to a pair of tiny, boot-clad feet.

The doorbell rang again.

Talk about lousy timing.

"Aren't you going to answer it?" her mother asked.

Like I have a choice. Mallory opened the door.

Brody's proportions reverted to normal, if size-twelve feet could be considered normal. "Well, hi."

"Hi." Despite her weakened physical state—or perhaps because of it—her heart fluttered madly. She really hadn't expected to see him again before the rehearsal dinner on Friday. After the way she'd acted Monday night, she wouldn't have been surprised if he'd called off the charade altogether.

"Aren't you going to ask me in?" Funny. He looked even more dangerous when he smiled. Her mother was going to flip out for sure when she saw that hair.

Sighing, she pulled the door wide. "Sure. Come in."

"Have you seen an Indian-head penny? An 1862 Indian-head penny? I think maybe I lost it in the shuffle the other night."

"What shuffle?" Her mother didn't miss a thing.

Mallory collapsed in the armchair and waved Brody to the couch. She pulled her legs up in a semifetal position and decided she was in dire need of an aspirin. Or two. Although, three might do the trick.

Brody addressed her mother. "I tried to turn a good-night kiss into something more and Mallory knocked me for a Fruit Loop."

"Good grief!" April plucked at the neck of her blouse as if she were choking.

Brody grinned. "You gotta admire her spunk. Unfortunately, I lost my lucky penny in the confusion."

"Why did you really drop by?" Mallory asked after her mother had left.

"What makes you think I didn't lose my lucky penny? As hard as you dumped me, I could have."

"Did you?"

He pulled the coin from his pocket, flipped it into the air, then caught it. "No, but I didn't want to mention the real reason for my visit in front of your mother. It's police business. Unofficial."

"What does that mean? How can police business be unofficial?"

"Well, the Yano break-in isn't my case, so technically, it's none of my business. But I'd like to take an informal look around the house and yard, just to satisfy my own curiosity. Something about that night's been bugging me, but I haven't been able to put my finger on what. I thought maybe if I returned to the scene of the crime, it might jog my memory. You still have the keys?"

"Yes."

"You don't sound too thrilled."

"What's the point? You said it yourself. It's not even your case."

Brody leaned across the trunk to shove her glasses up her nose. "What's it gonna hurt?"

What's it gonna hurt? Brody had said. Ha! File that one under *famous last words*. They'd been inside the house for all of five minutes and she'd already broken two of her fake nails. Mr. Edouard was going to have a major hissy fit.

"Picture the room as it looked before the break-in. Then tell me what's different now. Not just what's missing, but what's changed too."

Mallory obediently closed her eyes for a few seconds, then opened them and recited, "Silver's missing from the sideboard. That's it. There may be other stuff missing from drawers. I don't know what was in them to start with."

"Okay. Good." But he didn't say it with conviction. He frowned off into space, tapping his fingertips on the edge of the table. "They hit houses only when the owners are out of town. So how do they know who's out of town when?"

"Some postal worker is tipping them off," Mallory suggested.

Brody shook his head. "Thought of that, but they all checked out fine."

"Someone from the *Gazette* circulation desk?"

"No, we checked that too. We checked utilities. We checked lawn-care service providers. We checked cleaning ladies. We even checked travel agencies. And we came up empty. Any more suggestions?"

"What about the Dairy-Best man?"

"Who?"

"The Dairy-Best man. You know. Big yellow trucks. They deliver milk, ice cream, stuff like that. Nobody's going to want milk delivered when they're not home to drink it."

"The Yanos are Dairy-Best customers? You're sure of that?"

"Positive. Alex, Mrs. Yano, is addicted to their

Fudgie-Pudgies. Big, thick chocolate ice-cream sandwiches," she explained in response to Brody's puzzled
look. "She has a standing order, a box a week."

Brody looked thoughtful. "You just might be onto
something."

She chewed one of her ragged fingernails. "Are you
about done here?"

"Almost."

"Then I'll wait outside," she said.

As Brody made his way upstairs Mallory slipped out
the French doors. She sat on the steps of the back deck,
idly digging at the shredded bark of the planting bed
with the heel of one running shoe. Sunlight and peace
soothed her as Brody's projected few minutes stretched
to half an hour. Her muscles relaxed. Her headache
eased. She was almost asleep when she heard the sound
of his approaching footsteps. Lifting her leaden eyelids,
she glanced up with a yawn. "Find anything?"

"Nope." He dropped down beside her. "Didn't
really expect to. The team does a good job on crime
scenes. I knew they probably hadn't missed anything,
but"—he shrugged—"you never know. Wait a minute.
What's this?" He plucked a key from the base of a big
chunk of petrified wood where Mallory had disturbed
the shredded-bark ground cover.

"An extra key for the back door?"

"Damned stupid place to leave it. Almost as bad as
under a flowerpot."

Mallory cringed.

"Practically the first place the bad guys look after
they check under the mat and over the door." He
slipped the key back where he'd found it, hiding it with a
layer of bark.

"I guess our unofficial police search wasn't a complete bust, though. You have a new lead to check out. Dairy-Best."

"Thanks to you," he said, lifting one of her hands in his.

She shivered even though the sunshine was warm on her back.

"You don't have to be frightened of me, Mallory. I'm not going to hurt you."

"I know." She stared fixedly at the cedar decking.

"Then why the shudder?"

"On an intellectual level, I recognize that you're one of the good guys"—he squeezed her fingers—"but on a purely instinctive level, I'm still wary." She tried to pull free, but he tightened his grip. "Let go," she said, breathing unevenly.

"Not yet. Look at me."

Slowly she raised her gaze to meet his.

"Who did this to you, Mallory?"

She couldn't tell him. Even if she wanted to, her mouth wouldn't form the words. She couldn't think about it, let alone talk about it. Turning away, she shook her head.

Brody's hands gentled on hers. His voice softened. "I don't mean to upset you."

"I'm not upset." But she knew her protest wasn't very convincing, particularly when paired with the trembling of her fingers.

Brody released her hand. "I'm starved, and no wonder. It's after two. How about some lunch?"

"My stomach—" Mallory started. "I drank a few too many wine coolers last night."

"Oh?"

"Kyle and I were watching videos and feeling sorry for ourselves. He just broke up with his significant other. Again."

"Oh." He paused. "I can see I'm going to have to have a little talk with Kyle."

Meaning? She frowned and felt her glasses slide down her nose.

Smiling, Brody shoved them back up where they belonged. "If you're queasy, though, soup ought to fix you right up."

"I tried a cracker this morning, but it turned on me."

"The soup won't. I guarantee you'll feel a hundred percent better after you eat." He stood, stuffing his hands in his back pockets.

She shook her head. "Not now, Brody. I'm a mess. I need a shower and some serious time with a toothbrush and dental floss. My mouth tastes like well-used kitty litter."

He studied her in silence for a long moment. "Okay, but I'll stop by again this evening. Say, seven? Maybe you'll feel more human by then."

Just before five Brody got a tip from a pawnbroker on North Oregon Street, reporting a couple of suspicious-acting customers. He barreled down to the pawnshop, hoping for a break in the burglary case, but it turned out to be a pair of gangbangers who were trying to pawn half a dozen CD players they'd ripped off from the electronics shop two doors down.

The paperwork took a while. He thought about calling Mallory to say he might be delayed, but then a dispatcher reported that a truck and trailer rig had jackknifed nearby, causing a multiple-car pileup.

Brody drove out to make sure the truck driver didn't get cut loose before he was given a drug test, and forgot everything else when he saw the carnage at the scene of the accident. Two fatalities and eight others injured, including three in critical condition and one six-year-old who was Life-Flighted to Boise.

About seven-thirty someone shoved a corn dog and a cup of coffee at him, reminding him of his dinner date with Mallory. He called to explain the delay and was relieved when she sounded more groggy than angry.

So it was a shock to arrive on her doorstep at nine to find her lights off. He was just about to lean on the doorbell for the third time when he noticed an envelope with his name on it clipped to the top of the mailbox. He ripped open the note and squinted at the fine writing, edging closer to the streetlight to make out the words.

Dear Brody, she'd written. *Kyle was depressed and I was bored. We're at the Blue Russian.* She hadn't signed it or added any of those cutesy *X*s and *O*s. Of course, maybe she wasn't the *X*s and *O*s type. Just because she'd left a stilted note, it didn't necessarily mean she was ticked.

Yeah, right. His gut twisted. She was ticked. And no wonder. He was two hours late. He glanced at his watch. Two hours and seven minutes, to be exact. Hell, candy and flowers wouldn't cut it this time.

Even at a quarter after nine on a Thursday night, the Blue Russian was crowded. "Looking for someone, Detective?"

Brody recognized the owner, Dimitri Ivanovich. His

secluded home on Arrowhead Heights had been one of the first targeted by the burglary ring. "A friend of mine, Kyle Brewster." Brody could have asked for Mallory, but figured Ivanovich was more likely to know a regular.

"Ah, yes." A faint smile played around the corners of the Russian's thin, aristocratic mouth. Rumored to have been a rising star in the ballet world before a knee injury destroyed his dreams of becoming the next Baryshnikov, Ivanovich had emigrated to America. He'd taken to capitalism like a duck to water and had the Armani suits and Rolex watches to prove it.

Ivanovich raised an eyebrow. "He is expecting you, yes?"

"He asked me to meet him here."

The Russian shrugged. "I believe you will find your friend at the table in the far corner . . . with a young lady." His nose twitched almost imperceptibly.

"Another friend," Brody said, and made his way toward them. Tim the bartender was flirting madly with a glassy-eyed Kyle while Mallory broke pretzels into crumb-sized pieces.

"Well, hey!" Tim was the first to notice him. "If it isn't déjà vu all over again!"

"Pull up a chair." Kyle's gesture was overly precise. If Brody hadn't known him so well, he wouldn't have realized how drunk his friend was.

Mallory didn't even look up. Instead, she chose another mutilation victim from the bowl of pretzels. "Better late than never."

Not just ticked. Steamed. Which of his body parts would she mangle once the pretzel bowl was empty? Sorry seemed inadequate but he said it anyway, then asked Tim to bring him a beer.

"So," he said when the bartender moved off, "what's up?"

"I'm thinking about moving." Kyle studied the table-top as if it were a map. "What do you think of Seattle?"

"Great if you like rain."

"San Francisco?"

"Earthquakes."

"L.A.?"

"Smog."

"Phoenix?"

"Too damn hot. Look, if it's city life you crave, what's wrong with Boise?"

"Dolph's moving to Boise." Kyle infused the words with the same drama someone else might have used for, "Killer bees just attacked downtown Brunswick and they're headed this way."

"Who's Dolph?"

Kyle didn't answer, seemingly preoccupied once again with the invisible map.

Mallory frowned and shook her head.

Tim brought Brody's beer, then gathered up the empty glasses. "Another round here?"

"I don't think so," said Mallory. "I'm about ready to call it a night. What do you say, Kyle?"

He frowned. "I've heard Denver's nice."

SEVEN

"Sorry I was so late tonight." Brody smiled at Mallory across the table at Wong's, where they were finishing up a belated dinner.

"You said that already." She wasn't irritated anymore, but still thought he ought to suffer a little, just on general principle. "What's your problem anyway?"

"You mean, what's the deep, underlying reason for my chronic lateness? My mom used to swear I couldn't tell the big hand from the little hand."

"Maybe she should have bought you a digital watch."

"She did." He grinned sheepishly. "The truth is, nine times out of ten I'd come home after school to an empty house. Mom would be running one of the other kids to baseball practice or a dentist appointment or something. And I'd be alone. So I quit coming straight home. I'd mess around until I was pretty sure someone was there, waiting for me." He shrugged. "I never verbalized it before. Sounds pretty dumb, huh?"

"No, we all have our little quirks." Or in her case, a great big quirk.

"I really am sorry, though. I should have called earlier. Next time I will."

Next time. Mallory tried to ignore the implication, but it was hard not to think about possibilities with Brody smiling at her, his eyes soft, his expression tender. She shifted her gaze to the tabletop. Much more of this and she'd be inviting him back to her house for a nightcap.

Brody picked up the bill. "Are you ready?"

"Anytime." She slipped into her coat and gathered her things together as he went to pay the cashier.

Outside, the warmth of the afternoon was a distant memory. Mallory hugged her coat around her, thankful the wind wasn't blowing. She climbed into the Jeep on the passenger's side while Brody strapped himself into the driver's seat.

Brody frowned at the cars backed up behind the red light across from the mall entrance at Fourth and Verde. "Damn! That's the pickup. I swear to God, that's the same pickup."

"The one that's registered to the little old man?"

"Arlo Davis. Right. The one I'm pretty sure was used as the getaway vehicle in the Yano robbery. Fasten your seat belt, Mallory."

She shot him a startled look. "We're going to chase him?"

"We're going to tail him. With any luck he won't even know we're riding his bumper."

Okay, so he had a problem with chronic tardiness. At least he wasn't a dull date. She gripped the edge of her seat tightly as Brody threw the four-wheel drive into reverse and backed out of the parking space next to the restaurant with more speed than caution. He shifted into first and sped to the exit where he flicked on his right-turn signal.

"Shouldn't you call for backup?"

"I'm not planning to arrest anyone. I only want to catch a glimpse of the driver." The light changed and traffic began to move, but both westbound lanes were full of cars. Mallory kept her eye on the gray pickup, gaining speed now that it was through the light.

Suddenly Brody dove into traffic, bullying his way into a gap Mallory judged inadequate by a minimum of two feet. If the driver of the green BMW behind them hadn't stood on his brakes, he'd have rear-ended them.

"Can you see him?" asked Brody.

"Clear as a bell. He just made a very rude finger gesture."

"What?"

Mallory jerked her head toward the BMW behind them. "I think he's irritated."

"Forget him. I'm talking about the pick—" He broke off abruptly. "Damn, where'd he go?"

"There he is," Mallory said. "Up near Bi-Mart. He just turned right."

"Hell!" Brody slammed the steering wheel with the side of his fist as they got stuck behind a red light.

Mallory suspected he would have run the stoplight if they hadn't been three cars back.

The light changed and traffic moved forward. Brody cut into the left lane, passing the two cars ahead of him, then switching back into the outside lane.

Mallory noticed the green BMW was still on their tail. Its driver, a thin, bald guy with glasses, was driving one-handed while talking on a cellular phone. Not a smart move in her opinion. Not with the traffic this heavy.

The light at the T-intersection near Bi-Mart turned amber, but Brody didn't hesitate. Flipping on his signal, he took the corner wide, barely missing a big old boat of a Caddie that was hanging half over into their lane, waiting for a left turn.

"I don't see them," she said. The parking lot was full of pickups, but none of them was gray with a matching canopy.

"Damn!" Brody pulled into a parking space. A Brunswick Police Department cruiser pulled up on one side and the green BMW sandwiched them in on the other.

"Yo, Cesar. What's up, man?" Brody rolled down his window to greet the patrolman. "Mallory, say hey to Cesar Rios, one of Brunswick's finest."

"We've met. Cesar works out at the same gym I do."

"Mallory." Cesar shifted his Latin charm into overdrive, caressing each syllable of her name. "You're looking good. Haven't seen you in a while, pretty lady."

Mallory smiled. Cesar's flattery might be a little heavy-handed, but he was a thoroughly nice guy.

Though obviously Brody didn't agree. He scowled at his fellow officer as if he were an ax murderer in disguise. "Socialize on your own time, Rios. Did you notice a gray Ford pickup turn down Gleason?"

"No, actually I was trolling for speeders when a call came in."

"My call!" The bald man erupted from the BMW and marched around the rear of the Jeep just as Brody and Mallory were getting out. "Maniac!" He glared at

Brody. "Officer, I demand that you arrest this man!" He jabbed a finger in Brody's direction. Not the same one he'd used earlier.

The corners of Cesar's mouth twitched as if he were having a hard time keeping a straight face. "On what charge, sir?"

"Reckless endangerment? Operating a vehicle under the influence of intoxicants? Driving like a moron? How the hell should I know?" The little man was so angry, he was hopping from foot to foot like an agitated sparrow. "You're the cop, dammit!"

Brody rose to his full six-three. Towering over the little man, he flashed his badge. "So am I."

"Oh, yeah?" The man frowned, huffing and puffing as he assimilated the information. "Well, *Officer*, that badge doesn't give you the right to drive like a maniac. You damned near got all of us killed, pulling onto Fourth Avenue like a drunken idiot."

"I'm sorry. I was pursuing a suspect in a burglary."

"Yeah, right! Tell it to the judge." He smirked. "My brother-in-law's a lawyer. You'll be hearing from us."

Mallory stared after the green BMW. "I thought for sure that guy was going to make a citizen's arrest."

"Oh, yeah. That would have been the icing on the cake." A frown furrowed Brody's forehead. "Regan's gonna love this. Probably volunteer to testify against me."

Cesar chuckled. "Whassup, man? She still holding a grudge because you made detective instead of her?"

"To put it mildly."

"Fact is, the brass wouldn't have picked her anyway."

Cesar chewed at a toothpick he pulled from his pocket. "Hell, man. Even I had a better chance. Armstrong's sharp, but she's so damned unpredictable, has a real problem with her temper."

Brody grunted. "And meanwhile the gray pickup's long gone. I just wanted to get close enough to ID the driver. Thought I might catch a glimpse of the guy who got away the other night."

Cesar nodded. "The one who tried to crush your skull. Yeah, I heard about that. Damn good thing you got all those rocks in your head."

Brody ignored Cesar's good-natured insult, seemingly preoccupied with his own gloomy thoughts. His expression sent a ripple of apprehension down Mallory's spine even though she knew his anger wasn't directed toward her. "So what do we do now?" she asked.

"I go reset my speed trap." Cesar twirled an invisible mustache.

Brody shrugged. "And we go drag the gut a few times. If we get real lucky, we might run across that pickup again."

"Drag the gut?" What the heck was that supposed to mean?

Cesar grinned at her confusion. "Local cop lingo," he explained, "for cruising the truck route." He turned to Brody, nodding thoughtfully. "Yeah, man. Sounds *real* romantic."

Mallory punched the buttons on the car stereo in vain, searching for a station that played something other than country or rap.

"I see him." Brody tensed at the wheel.

"Where?"

"He just pulled onto Oregon Street three cars ahead of us. Two people in the front seat. If you squint, you can see the silhouettes of their heads through the canopy window."

"What do we do now?"

"Just keep an eye on them, see where they go."

"What if they turn off?"

"Then we turn off too. Don't worry." He reached across to give her hand a squeeze. "If I thought there was any danger, I wouldn't involve you."

Mallory's stomach gave a lurch, but she wasn't concerned about the possible risks involved in what they were doing. What bothered her was the way her heart beat out of control in response to the light pressure of Brody's fingers. *Don't do this to yourself, idiot.* Nothing would come of it. Nothing could come of it.

"I wonder where the heck he's headed," she said. "He's passed a grocery store, two gas stations, four fast-food joints, a Laundromat, a video rental place, and the liquor store. What else is open this late?"

The pickup signaled for a left turn, changed lanes, then pulled into the turn lane across from the Blue Russian. "A bar," said Brody.

"Aren't we going to follow?"

"Not just yet. Too obvious. We'll go on up a little way and come back down the alley."

The alley was unpaved and largely unlit. A couple of the bigger potholes threatened to swallow the Jeep completely. Brody swung around onto the paved parking lot of the Blue Russian just as the driver of the pickup was stepping inside the bar.

"Well, well, well. Our friend from the Yano robbery," Brody said in satisfaction. "I'd know those hulking shoulders anywhere. That old coot, Davis, was lying through his teeth. Wonder what *his* connection is?"

"Maybe he doesn't have one. Maybe the big guy took the truck without Arlo Davis's knowledge." Mallory shrugged. "What's got me curious is what a big ol' bubba like that is doing here. The Blue Russian isn't exactly a redneck hangout."

"Maybe I ought to go inside and find out."

Brody's voice held a hint of steel. The hairs on Mallory's arms stood up in response. "You're not going to start anything, are you?"

"Why would I do that? Just because that guy's the one who most likely coldcocked me, then stuffed me in that stinking Dumpster? Hell, I can take a joke."

"Brody, I'm serious. You already found out what you wanted to know. Bubba has access to the truck you saw at Denny's, despite anything Mr. Arlo 'Upstanding Citizen' Davis may say to the contrary."

He scowled at the pickup. "True, but I'd still like to know what the hell he's up to in there."

"Fine, go check it out. If you pick a fight, though, he'll realize you're onto him. Why tip your hand before you have enough evidence to arrest him? That doesn't make any sense."

A reluctant smile nudged the corners of Brody's mouth. "What makes you so smart?"

"Years of experience dealing with hotheaded eleven-year-olds."

"Guess I better watch it, huh?" Brody's smile widened to a full-fledged grin. "If I were to start a fight on top of those two tardies—"

"Three tardies."

"Okay, on top of those *three* tardies, I'd get detention for sure. Which might not be so bad—not if you're the one in charge of my punishment."

"You're impossible."

"No, I'm not." He shoved her glasses up her nose. "Not impossible at all."

A tenuous thread of awareness stretched between them. Mallory held her breath, waiting. For a second she thought Brody was going to kiss her, and knew if he did, they'd both regret it.

Perhaps he saw the panic in her eyes and changed his mind. Or perhaps he'd never intended to kiss her in the first place. But in any event, all he did was flash a quick smile and say, "I'm going to slip inside and see if I can figure out what the big guy's up to."

She released her pent-up breath in a sigh and swallowed hard. "Mind if—" Her voice came out in a squeak. She swallowed again and gave it another try. "Mind if I tag along?"

Brody shook his head. "I'd rather you stayed out here. Davis is the only one we saw go inside. His passenger may still be in the truck. I need you to keep an eye on the pickup."

"If the pickup leaves, am I supposed to follow?"

"No, just pay attention to which way it goes."

"Okay. This might even be fun," Mallory said with a smile. "I can pretend I'm a TV detective pulling surveillance."

"Don't get your hopes up," Brody warned. "Real-life surveillance isn't as exciting as the Hollywood version. If you get bored, feel free to listen to the radio." And with that, he followed Davis inside.

Guys have all the fun, Mallory decided ten minutes

later. She sat sideways in her seat, staring fixedly at the tailgate of the pickup. Like gawking at the bumper stickers was doing any good. She sighed in frustration. From here she couldn't see the person in the passenger's seat. She couldn't even see what, if anything, was hidden under the canopy. Of course, if she were to wander casually over there and maybe glance inside on her way past . . .

Mallory was out of the Jeep before she'd completed the thought. She shut her door quietly, glancing around to be sure no one was watching.

The pickup was squeezed into one of the narrow slots that edged the front of the long, low building. Brody had parked in one of the wider diagonal spaces on the east side of the small lot. Mallory cut across the pavement, thankful that she'd worn her sneakers. The rubber soles were perfect for furtive operations.

She made a beeline for the rear of the gray pickup, peering intently into the canopy before turning to cut between the truck and the burgundy car parked beside it.

The back end was full of something. What, she couldn't say, since canvas tarps covered the contents, hiding them from view. Disappointing, but not really surprising. What crook worth his salt drove around town with the evidence of his crime on display?

What was surprising was the identity of Davis's passenger. He'd been lying down on the seat, but when he heard Mallory's soft footsteps, he jerked erect, and she found herself staring into a pair of big brown eyes.

A black Lab, the owner of the big brown eyes, opened his jaws in a doggy smile and woofed a soft greeting.

"Great watchdog you are, buddy."

The Lab pressed his nose against the window, gazing

at her wistfully. Bubba hadn't impressed her, but his dog was a born charmer.

"You're a darling," she told him, "but I don't have time to pl . . ." Her words died away as she noticed what the dog was leaning against—a perfectly ordinary navy-blue duffel bag that wouldn't have surprised her a bit if it hadn't been for the red-and-black-lace-trimmed garter belt partially caught in the zipper.

Women's underwear. Guess that might explain what a redneck like Bubba was doing at the Blue Russian. But oh, boy. The thought of Bubba in a garter belt boggled her mind.

Caught off guard, Mallory nearly had a heart attack as the door of the Blue Russian flew open and two men came out. One was the owner, the other, Bubba. So where the heck was Brody? she wondered, worried. Out back in the trash bin?

Before the two men had a chance to turn her direction, she ducked out of sight, flattening herself on the pavement and squeezing under the burgundy car.

Her heart slammed so loudly against the wall of her chest, she was half-afraid the men would hear it. Two pairs of shoes marched past her nose. The owner's well-polished oxblood loafers offered quite a contrast to Davis's scuffed work boots, making it easy to tell the two apart even from this vantage point.

"What are you doing here?" The speaker's voice was deep and faintly accented. The owner. Dimitri, Kyle had called him. "Not too bright using the old man's truck again."

"Oh, he don't notice nothin'. Besides, I needed it. The boss asked me to run some errands." This voice was coarser to match the run-over heels and knotted leather shoestrings of Davis's work boots.

"I'm busy, Arlo. What's the problem?"

Arlo? As in Arlo Davis? Were there two of them? An Arlo Senior and an Arlo Junior perhaps?

"The boss sent some stuff over. Says he ain't got room for it."

"Storage isn't part of the deal. I've got too many nosy employees."

"But the boss said—"

"All right, dammit. But bring it around to the rear. No need to advertise."

Dimitri stomped back inside and Arlo circled the truck and got in on the driver's side.

Where the heck was Brody?

She slid cautiously across the rough pavement and out from under the car on the opposite side, crouching down between the next two cars.

She waited until the pickup had backed out of its space and eased around toward the rear of the building before she ran across the lot to Brody's Jeep.

"Where were you?" he demanded as she piled in on the passenger's side.

Mallory nearly jumped out of her skin. "I thought you were still inside. How did you get here?" She took a couple of deep breaths in an effort to slow her adrenaline-charged heart. "I didn't see you leave the bar."

"I slipped out the side door." Brody frowned. "But you didn't answer my question. Where were you? I thought I told you to stay in the Jeep."

"No, actually you asked me to keep an eye on the pickup. Which I did, turning up some very interesting evidence in the process."

"Stupid move." Brody was tight-lipped. His frown had grown into a full-fledged scowl. "What if the passenger had caught you snooping around?"

"I'm not an idiot, Brody. I was careful to make the whole thing look natural. And as it happened, it didn't matter since the passenger is a dog."

"A dog? As in woof-woof?"

"Yeah, a big black Labrador. Nice, friendly pooch."

"Okay, you got lucky. There was no second man. But what if Bubba had caught you poking around? He wasn't inside more than fifteen minutes."

"He almost did catch me. I had to hide under a car."

Brody swore.

"I'm sorry. I wasn't thinking about the possible danger. And right now that's beside the point. We're wasting time. As we speak, they're probably unloading all the stolen goods."

"What stolen goods?"

"Arlo said—"

"Arlo?"

"That's what the Russian called him. Confused the heck out of me too. Anyway, while I was hiding I overheard their entire conversation." She did a quick recap. "So you see, we're wasting time. We should be sneaking around to the alley to keep tabs on them."

"That conversation doesn't prove a thing. I have a hard time believing Ivanovich is involved. Hell, his place was one of the first the burglars hit."

"Clever, huh? Who'd suspect one of the victims?" She shrugged. "I told you what they said. Feel free to draw your own conclusions, but my guess is they're disposing of the evidence as we speak."

"Maybe you're right. It's worth checking out anyway."

Mallory started to get out of the Jeep, but Brody stopped her. "Aren't we going to go see what's happening out back?"

"Not until I call for backup." He put through a call to the dispatcher on his car phone. "Damn," he muttered as he hung up.

"What's wrong?"

"She gave me an ETA of ten minutes. All patrolmen busy at present." He smacked the steering wheel, then checked his watch. Swearing softly under his breath, he got out of the Jeep. Mallory started to follow, but he stopped her with a shake of his head. "No, you keep an eye peeled for a cruiser. Tell them I'm out back."

"Should you be doing this alone?"

"No, but I don't seem to have a choice. Don't worry. I'm just going to watch. I won't make a move without backup."

And he would have followed through on that promise, only by the time he got around back, the truck was deserted, the tailgate hanging open. No Dimitri Ivanovich. No Arlo Bubba Bo Bob Davis. And as far as Brody could tell, no evidence either.

Swearing under his breath, he lurked in the shadow of a steel storage shed. Hell, even if a uniform showed up this minute, they couldn't prove zip. And he'd bet his pension Dimitri Ivanovich wasn't going to invite them to have a look around inside without a search warrant. Dammit, what now?

He heard a noise behind him, the rattle of a rock

skittering across the strip of concrete connecting the shed with the Blue Russian itself. He started to turn but barely made it a quarter of the way around before something solid connected painfully with the back of his head.

Mallory watched and waited as the minutes crawled by with agonizing slowness. This was far worse than her earlier stint of surveillance. At least then she'd had something to keep an eye on. Now all she had to stare at was the second hand on her watch.

Hadn't Brody said his backup was due in ten minutes. It had been almost fifteen. Fourteen and a half, to be exact. So where the heck were they?

A patrol car appeared so suddenly, it was almost as if she'd conjured it up from the depths of her imagination. Though if she truly had been doing the conjuring, she'd have produced Cesar Rios instead of Officer Regan Armstrong. Armstrong parked next to the Jeep, so close Mallory couldn't open her door without scraping the insignia off the cruiser's driver's-side door.

Officer Armstrong rolled down her window, motioning for Mallory to do the same. Then she deliberately shone her flashlight in Mallory's face. "Where's Hunter?"

"Could you shift that light out of my eyes, please?"

Armstrong moved the beam an inch or so to the left. "I said, where's Hunter?"

"He went around back to keep an eye on the pickup." Mallory explained what she'd overheard. "Only I'm beginning to get worried," she added. "He's been gone almost twenty minutes."

"Damn hotshot. Should have waited for backup."

"He *was* waiting for backup. All he intended to do was watch, not apprehend. What took you so long anyway?"

"Look, lady, don't question how I do my job."

Mallory opened her mouth to let Officer Armstrong know exactly what she could do with her job, then thought better of it. Alienating Brody's backup was not a brilliant idea.

"Around back you say?" Armstrong asked.

"Right."

Without another word, Officer Armstrong doused her flashlight, rolled up her window, and started her engine.

"Wait! I'm going too!"

Either she didn't hear Mallory's shout or she wasn't interested in company. She backed out of her parking slot and drove around the side of the building into the alley.

"Charming," Mallory muttered. She rolled her own window up, then hopped out of the Jeep to follow on foot.

Officer Armstrong had parked her squad car so it blocked both the alley and access to the alley from the parking lot. When Mallory came around the end of the Blue Russian, she saw the policewoman standing under the security light near the back door, hands on hips, frowning at the No Parking sign tacked to the wall. She turned at the sound of Mallory's approach. "This place is deserted."

Nothing like stating the obvious, Mallory thought.

"So where's the pickup?" Armstrong demanded.

"More importantly, where's Brody?"

"Out hotdogging it, no doubt. Detective Hunter's a born hero." Armstrong made it sound like a disease.

"Maybe. Maybe not. Have you looked for him?"

The redhead shrugged. "Looked for him where? There aren't a hell of a lot of places to hide back here."

"The shed?"

"Locked," said Armstrong. "Ditto the back door. No bushes. No trees. No place to hide. Except . . ."

Both of them noticed the big blue trash bin on the far side of the shed at the same time.

"Oh, jeez. Not the Dumpster." Mallory stumbled over to it on legs that seemed to have turned to rubber. She banged on the side. "Brody! Are you in there, Brody?" she asked, hoping he wasn't. After her last experience, she wasn't anxious to look but knew she had to.

There weren't any sandbags on top this time and she managed to lift the heavy cover by herself. It fell back, connecting with the wall of the shed with a resounding clang. "Brody?"

"Did you find him?" Officer Armstrong moved up beside her and shone her flashlight inside. The Dumpster was empty except for some flattened boxes and Brody Hunter.

Mallory's partially digested shrimp fried rice burned its way back up her esophagus. What had Tim said earlier? Déjà vu all over again? Only this time the red stuff wasn't tomato sauce. "Call an ambulance," she managed to say before being very, very sick all over Officer Armstrong's shiny black shoes.

EIGHT

Mallory had been relieved to discover Brody's injuries weren't as serious as they'd first appeared. He'd come to before the ambulance arrived, more mad than hurt, furious that he'd taken another blow from an unseen assailant. "With head wounds you always bleed like a stuck hog," he'd told Mallory. "I swear, when I catch up with this joker, I'm gonna stick him in a trash bin and see how the hell he likes it."

"At least this Dumpster didn't stink like the other one," Mallory'd said, her comment earning her a disgusted look.

After giving Officer Armstrong his statement, Brody'd been rushed off to Brunswick General. Mallory had stayed behind to answer a few more questions, then trailed the ambulance to the hospital in Brody's Jeep.

She entered the emergency room through the automatic doors and approached the woman behind the admitting desk. With iron-gray hair permed to a frazzle and the poker-stiff posture that suggested a military background, she was what Mallory's father would have described as a starchy old trout. Busy attacking the keyboard of her computer as if she had a grudge against it, she didn't even glance up at Mallory's approach.

"Excuse me?" Mallory said.

The receptionist glared at her. "Hang on. I'm almost done." She bashed away, *clickety-click*, for another minute or two before looking up again, this time with what was probably meant to be a smile, though Mallory's first thought was: Grandma, what big teeth you have!

"I'm here to see Brody Hunter. An ambulance brought him in half an hour ago. Head injury."

"You a relative?"

"No."

The woman's face closed up. "Then I'm afraid—"

"I'm a friend," Mallory said quickly. "Close friend. Fiancée, in fact." She jammed her left hand into the pocket of her jacket to hide its ringless state.

The woman's disbelieving stare probably would have intimidated most people. Fortunately, Mallory was used to her mother, and by comparison, this receptionist was a marshmallow.

"Where is he?" She peered over the woman's shoulder into the emergency room proper, where white- and green-clad figures rushed back and forth like industrious ants.

The receptionist pointed heavenward and Mallory's heart gave a lurch, even though she was positive Brody's injuries hadn't been serious enough to send him to the pearly gates. "Second floor," the woman said. She checked her clipboard. "X-ray department."

Mallory heard Brody the instant she stepped off the

elevator. No doubt the rest of Brunswick could hear him too.

She found him in a waiting room at the end of a long, empty corridor. The scene was like something from *One Flew over the Cuckoo's Nest*. Two LPNs held him on one side, two orderlies on the other, while an RN, a statuesque brunette built along the lines of an Amazon, strapped him to the gurney. And the whole time Brody was yelling, his language foul enough to bring a blush to a truck driver's cheek.

"What is going on here?"

The tableau froze at the sound of her voice. Everyone stared at her, including Brody, his harangue halted in mid-epithet.

He soon found his tongue, however. "Mallory, tell these officious morons they can't keep me here against my will. I have rights, and that includes the right to check myself the hell out of this damn torture chamber."

"Not until you have the X rays Dr. Yamamoto ordered." The nurse fastened the last restraint and the others took a wary step back as Brody lunged against his bonds.

"You're not keeping him overnight for observation?" He must have lost half a pint of blood. What was wrong with these people?

Brody and the nurse both glared at her. "That was the original plan," the nurse said, "but he's right. We can't keep him if he doesn't want to stay, and by the looks of him, I'd say he doesn't have a concussion, anyway. Still, it's not my call. The doctor's the one who ordered the pictures, and Mr. Uncooperative here isn't leaving until he gets them." Hands on hips, she turned her glare back on Brody. "If you don't calm down and quit swearing, I'm going to personally wash your mouth out with soap. And if that doesn't do the trick"—she grinned evilly—"I can arrange for an enema."

Brody scowled. "I bet you would, Nurse Ratched."

"That's Nurse Ratcliff. And you can make book on it, buster." She turned back to Mallory. "By the way, who are you, and what are you doing here?"

"I'm his . . ." Fiancée, she started to say, but remembered in time about her ringless left hand, now resting on Brody's shoulder in plain sight of God and everybody. "His sister."

Nurse Ratcliff narrowed her eyes. "You two don't look alike."

"Different mothers," said Mallory.

"Different fathers," said Brody at the same time. They exchanged a glance. "My father married her mother," he explained. "Technically, she's my stepsister."

Technically, he was a liar.

The nurse evidently thought so too. She didn't look convinced, but she let it pass. "Don't you people have work to do?" she asked the gawking staff members. As they shuffled away she addressed Mallory. "You've got about ten minutes before they're ready for him. See if you can reason with the big bozo. A night in the hospital isn't going to kill him, whereas if he rushes back out and gets knocked over the head again . . ." She shrugged. "You know what they say. Third time's a charm."

Mallory stared after the nurse's retreating back. What she meant was, nobody's skull could stand up to such punishment on a regular basis. Next time Brody might not be so lucky.

Mallory didn't realize her grip had tightened on

Brody's shoulder until he accused her of trying to cut off his circulation.

"Sorry," she said.

He looked up at her, one eyebrow raised. "Do you think Ratched was serious about the enema?"

Mallory laughed. "Dead serious. You'd better settle down. That is not a lady to mess around with."

"How about you, Mallory?" He grinned. "Can I mess around with you?"

"Whoa, boy. Off-limits. I'm your sister, remember?"

"Stepsister," he corrected. "No blood tie. Come on, honey. One little kiss. That's all I need. One little teensy-weensy kiss and I promise I'll be a good boy and not throw any more tantrums for Nurse Ratched."

"I don't think it's a good idea to get overstimulated in your condition."

"Then you'd better leave, sis, 'cause just being in the same room with you is enough to get me overstimulated."

Mallory studied him carefully. "Brody, are you sure you're all right? I think that knock on the head tweaked your brain."

"No, you're the one who tweaked my brain, honey. How about it? Kiss me?"

She wanted to. Oh, God, she wanted to, but she was afraid a kiss would only leave him wanting more. And more was something she didn't have to give.

"Just one kiss, Mallory. For luck. To ward off the possibility that Arlo Two might sneak in the back door and adjust the X-ray machine so it fries all my little gray cells."

"Fertile little gray cells. You have quite an imagination."

"Oh, Mallory, please. If the situation were reversed, I'd grant you one final wish."

"You're going to have some X rays, Hunter, not a lethal injection."

"I won't even kiss you back. Promise." His smile was irresistible.

Heck, he was right. One little kiss. What was the big deal? Mallory hitched herself up on the edge of the gurney and leaned toward Brody, stopping an inch from his mouth. "Close your eyes," she said. There was something very unnerving about being stared at, at such close range.

"I want to watch your expression."

"What's to see? Eyes closed. Lips puckered."

Brody didn't say a word, just continued to smile at her. Mallory felt the heat in her cheeks and knew she was blushing.

"Much more of this, Brody Hunter, and I'm going to tell the nurse you *requested* an enema."

"Kiss me," he said, his mouth so close, she could feel the warmth of his breath on her face.

Good thing she hadn't claimed to be his fiancée; he'd be insisting on a full-body massage.

"Kiss me," he said again. "Hurry. I think I hear the storm troopers coming."

Mallory heard them too.

She kissed him, a sweet, gentle pressure that shouldn't have caused her nipples to pucker or her groin muscles to tighten but did. She broke contact with a sigh and opened her eyes to see that Brody looked every bit as shell-shocked as she felt. She gave a little hiccup of laughter, embarrassed by her state of arousal. "I thought you were lying about not kissing me back."

"I was," he said. "That is, I meant to." He blinked. "Only I got distracted. Toss that blanket up over me, will you?"

"You're cold?"

He frowned. "Not exactly."

As Mallory reached down for the blanket she discovered the source of his discomfort straining against the center strap. "Oh," she said. She tucked the blanket over him loosely to disguise the embarrassing bulge seconds before the two orderlies entered the room.

"Thanks for waiting," Brody said as Mallory met him at the emergency-room exit an hour later.

"You're my ride home. What choice did I have?" She handed him the keys to the Jeep. "Besides, if I hadn't waited, I'd have missed the thrill of watching a late-night episode of *Star Trek* on the grainy thirteen-inch TV in the waiting room. The Tribbles episode, one of my favorites. Of course I had to fight a couple of off-duty maintenance men for the remote—they wanted to watch the Home Shopping Network—but I pretended I didn't understand English, jabbered at them in my best German until they backed off."

She examined him closely. He didn't look too worse for wear, other than some heavy-duty beard stubble, the bandage on the back of his head, and the hair straggling loose around his face. "How'd your X rays turn out?"

"I'll live."

"Want me to drive?"

"No, aside from an industrial-strength headache, I'm okay."

"Going to be feeling good enough to escort me to the rehearsal dinner tonight?"

"Oh, sure. Couple of aspirin and a few hours' sleep and I'll be fine. What time should I pick you up?"

"Dinner reservations at the Piccadilly Room are at seven, so why don't you pick me up about six-thirty? And please, Brody, be on time. My father gets very cranky when he isn't fed promptly."

"I'll be there," he said. "I owe you one."

"Two," she corrected him. "You owe me two."

Brody rang Mallory's doorbell at six-thirty on the dot, proud of himself because, for once, he wasn't late.

She opened the door and her big blue eyes widened in surprise. "You cut off your ponytail!"

"Had to. They shaved a patch in back where they put in the stitches. No way to cover it up. This way it blends in a little better. What do you think?"

She nodded thoughtfully. "I like it, and Mother will be thrilled. Come on in. I'm almost ready. I just have to slip into my dress." She went to change, leaving him to fend for himself in the living room.

Brody plopped down on the armchair and began leafing through the evening edition of the *Eastern Oregon Gazette*. The burglary ring had made the front page again, a house near the college their latest target, but it was the sidebar that caught his attention. "Mallory!"

"What?" she said from right behind him.

"Did you tell anyone about the Fudgie-Pudgie connection?" he demanded, turning around. Then he saw her, and all thoughts of the case flew right out of his head. "Holy cow," he muttered. An inadequate response, but the best his poor brain could produce under the circumstances. He'd always thought Mallory was beautiful. But tonight she was so gorgeous that she quite literally took his breath away.

"What's your honest opinion?" She twirled around to show off her new blue dress. The soft fabric clung to her curves, then flared to a full skirt that hit mid-thigh, baring what seemed to be miles of long, slender legs. The sleeves were long and snug, the neckline a deep U-shape that revealed more than a hint of cleavage. Her eyes were soft and dewy, her mouth pink and inviting, her hair silky and touchable. "Do I look like a frumpy loser of an old maid?"

Brody took a deep breath. "Not hardly. Poor Corby's going to kick himself clear into next week for being dumb enough to let you get away."

She smiled in satisfaction. "Good. That's the idea."

"I made a complete fool of myself, didn't I?" Mallory huddled in the passenger seat of the Jeep, looking miserable.

Brody had been driving the deserted back streets of Brunswick for the past twenty minutes to give her a chance to calm down, but his plan didn't seem to be working.

"You made a perfectly reasonable assumption."

"You mean I jumped to a bizarre—and totally erroneous—conclusion. How could I have believed for one instant that Evan was having a sleazy affair with Lamour Hooterman? I should have known better. I just wasn't thinking straight."

"What *was* he doing with her? I didn't quite catch that."

"Buying the house across the street from yours."

He glanced at her with a frown. "Now wait. I thought a middle-aged couple just bought it."

"They did, Lamour's parents. Only right after the deal closed, her father got transferred to Spokane, so Lamour's been showing the place to prospective buyers. Evan wasn't hiding an illicit affair; he was just afraid to tell Lindsey that he'd accepted KBRU's job offer and that they were moving back to Brunswick right after the honeymoon." She thunked her forehead with the heel of her hand. "How could I be so stupid?"

"I still say it was an understandable mistake."

"No, I mean how could I be so stupid that I let myself get involved in Evan and Lindsey's problems. I knew better." She sighed. "Now everybody's mad at me for causing a ruckus at the rehearsal dinner."

"Your dad's not mad at you. You should have heard him laugh when you dumped your drink over Corby's head."

Mallory grinned. "Evan was never Daddy's favorite person"—she chuckled—"and he did look pretty funny with wine dripping off the end of his nose."

Brody walked Mallory to her front door, but she didn't go inside right away. She leaned against the door, smiling up at him. "Thank you," she said, "for helping me see the humorous side of tonight's fiasco."

"No problem. I owed you one, remember?"

"Two," she said. "You owed me two." Her voice

sounded breathier than normal, which probably had a lot to do with the look on his face.

Brody's eyes glittered like coins in the moonlight. Even with his hair cut short, he looked dangerous. An anticipatory shiver rippled down her spine. He's going to kiss me, she thought, bracing herself for a gut-wrenching panic attack that never came.

Neither did the kiss.

"We need to talk, Mallory." His expression hadn't frightened her, but the husky undertones in his voice set off all her warning bells.

"What about?"

He flattened his palms against the siding on either side of her head and leaned in closer. "I think you know how attracted I am to you."

She caught a whiff of his aftershave, underlaid by something else, something that was pure, primitive male, a vivid reminder of his untimely arousal in the X-ray-department waiting room. She remembered, too, her own response.

Mallory tore her gaze from his. It was hard to think with Brody staring into her eyes as if he could see her thoughts mirrored there.

"Mallory, I'm attracted to you and I'm pretty sure you're attracted to me too."

"I—"

"So what's the problem? Granted, you don't flinch away from a casual touch anymore and you've kissed me a time or two, but I'd like to take our relationship another step. Only the one time I tried, I ended up flat on the welcome mat. Please, Mallory, we need to talk about it."

She frowned down at the keys clenched in her hands.

"You're right. I haven't played fair with you. Hot one minute, cold the next. No wonder you're confused. You deserve an explanation." Her voice faded away to a husky whisper. "I owe it to you, but . . ."

Brody nudged her glasses up her nose. "No, you owe it to yourself to talk this through."

Mallory turned away, ducking beneath his arm. "You don't understand."

"Then explain."

"Not tonight. I'm tired."

Brody grabbed her forearm. "Mallory . . ."

She trembled violently. "I can't talk about it."

He pulled her around to face him. "You have to talk about it, honey, and now is as good a time as any." He pulled her chin up so she was forced to look at him. "I'm not your enemy, you know. Dammit, Mallory, I think I'm falling in love with you."

Her heart fluttered wildly. She felt faint. "No, you can't!"

"Talk to me. Tell me what the problem is."

She closed her eyes against the entreaty in his face and drew a long, shuddering breath. He deserved the truth. She turned to the door, unlocked it, and shoved it open. "Come on in. It's cold out."

NINE

Mallory hadn't cringed when he sat down beside her on the love seat, a good sign, but she hadn't said anything yet, either, other than to offer him coffee, which he'd refused. She scowled at the antique trunk as if her personal demons were locked inside of it instead of her head. She spoke finally without looking up. "Did you have a special place when you were a kid?"

"The willows down by the river behind our house," he answered promptly, "where my stepbrothers and I played cops and robbers."

"My special place was Valley View Memorial Gardens, the cemetery on the hill across from the college."

"You played in a graveyard?" Brody suppressed a shudder. He'd never been fond of cemeteries himself.

"Don't tell me you're superstitious." A faint smile lit her face.

"Not superstitious. Just not too thrilled with graveyards. A little too Stephen King for my taste."

"The graves weren't the attraction." She frowned

again. "An irrigation ditch separates the old part of the cemetery from the new part. I loved splashing around in the water, even though it wasn't really deep enough for swimming."

Which sounded pretty innocuous. In which case, why was she bringing it up?

Mallory turned to face him. "I like you, Brody. I like you a lot, but there are things you don't know about me. I can't give you what you need."

The stricken expression on her face set his heart racing with fear. He knew that look. He'd seen one like it on Jenna's face the day she died. "Whatever it is, we can work it out."

Her smile held a tinge of bitterness. "Hear me out first before you make any rash promises." She drew another deep breath. "Like I said, Brody, I really like you, but I can't make love with you." She shuddered convulsively.

"Why? You and Corby—"

"No, we never . . ." She let it trail off. "I couldn't. I can't." She stared hard at her hands, braced on the edge of the trunk.

"I'm a patient man, Mallory. I can wait until you're ready."

"I—" She tried again. "You don't understand. I'll never be ready. I like you a lot, and I'm attracted to you, *very* attracted to you, but . . ." She trailed off again.

But not enough to take a chance. "I understand," he said, though he didn't.

Mallory gripped his hand in hers. "No, you don't, but I'll do my best to explain." She squeezed his fingers tightly and took a deep breath. Her face was pale. She trembled violently.

"Mallory, you don't have to tell me this if you don't want to."

She shushed him with an increased pressure on his hand.

"The summer I turned eleven . . ." She quavered to a halt, took another deep breath and started over. "The summer I turned eleven, I had a huge crush on Cameron Benson, who lived next door to us. When he got a summer job helping the caretaker at Valley View, I was in seventh heaven. He was six years older and completely out of my league, but that didn't matter. I was happy just to have the chance to watch him, to worship from afar."

His hand was going numb, but he didn't move, afraid if he broke her concentration, she might never again find the courage to speak.

"I spent hours spinning absurd and elaborate fantasies starring me as a feisty Princess Leia type and Cameron as Brunswick's answer to Harrison Ford." She turned away as if she were embarrassed by what she was telling him.

Brody squeezed her shoulder lightly. "Don't worry about it. Fantasizing is standard adolescent behavior. I seem to remember having a real serious thing for my eighth-grade English teacher, Miss Tremaine. She had long, dark hair, big brown eyes, and a voice that could make John Milton sound sexy."

Mallory turned to him, her face expressionless. "Normal," she said, "as long as it stays a fantasy." She bit her lip. "I thought the sun revolved around Cameron. He was a senior, popular, a football player, not to mention the handsomest boy in school." She drew a ragged breath. "By contrast, I was dorky little middle-school kid. A nobody. Part of the scenery.

"One sweltering July day Lindsey and I were splashing around in the ditch, trying to cool off, when I looked up and there he was. Cameron. Like a dream come true. He came driving across the grass on a big riding mower. He was wearing cutoffs. No shirt. I'd never seen anyone more gorgeous in my life." Her fingernails dug into his flesh.

Oh, God. Brody's guts twisted like a sack full of snakes. *Depths. Deep, dark, murky depths.*

"He looked up and saw me then, and he smiled and killed the mower. I remember the way his chest and shoulders looked, shiny with sweat, the way the sunlight reflected off the fuzzy blond hairs on his legs." She shivered. "He called me by name, and that surprised me because I didn't think he knew who I was. Just hearing him say my name was enough to give me goose bumps." She paused. When she continued, she spoke in a near whisper. "I was flattered, honored. None of it seemed real. It was like somehow I'd slipped inside one of my own daydreams."

Damn. The snakes in his gut coiled a little tighter. He knew what was coming.

"Lindsey asked if she could have a ride on the mower, but he said no, he needed to let it cool off for a while. Then he asked if we were hot. He told Lindsey he had some sodas in a cooler back at his pickup and asked if she'd like one. She said sure and took off for the other side of the cemetery. Then he offered to show me the secret room under the gazebo."

I'll just bet he did. Brody clenched his jaw and kept quiet. This was not the time to interrupt.

Mallory's eyes looked huge and unfocused, as if she had just awakened from a nightmare. "I had no idea what he intended, Brody. None. He was so nice, so friendly." She swallowed hard and fell silent.

Bastard, thought Brody. He gripped the edge of the love seat tightly with his free hand.

"There was a door hidden in the lattice and storage space underneath, not a room really. More like a dirt-floored crawl space, only it was tall enough to stand up in and there were all sorts of tools stacked inside. Buckets and hoses. Rakes, shovels. I didn't really pay much attention because as soon as he had the door shut, he started kissing me, and it was exactly like my fantasies." She bit her lip again. "At first."

Damn, he couldn't take any more. "The bastard raped you, didn't he?"

She frowned. "Sort of. I mean, now I can see that yes, it was rape, but then I thought the whole thing was my fault."

"*Your* fault!" Mallory flinched and Brody realized he'd shouted the words. "Your fault?" he repeated more quietly.

She averted her face, staring again at the trunk. "When Cameron kissed me, I kissed him back. And when he pushed me down in the dirt, I didn't say anything. I didn't scream or tell him to stop."

Brody's throat felt tight. "Because you didn't have a clue what he was up to."

"No." Her voice was tinged with bitterness. "But I should have. Only I'd spent too much time with my nose stuck in a book, and not enough time learning what happens to stupid little girls in real life." She drew a quick, sobbing breath.

"Oh, Mallory. I'm so sorry."

She shook her head slowly from side to side. "Cameron wasn't. He said I'd got what I deserved. He said any girl who went around in a wet T-shirt was just asking for it. He said I should be thanking him, not bawling like a damned baby. He said shut up or he'd knock my teeth down my throat and give me something to cry about."

Brody held her close. "Dammit. You *were* a baby, Mallory."

"With a grown-up's body." She shrugged his arm away, folded her legs up, and wrapped her arms around them, resting her cheek on her knees. "And I did flirt with him. Just a little. In the beginning."

Brody clenched his hands into fists. "How can you make excuses for an animal like that?"

"I'm just telling you what happened, Brody, so you'll understand why I'm the way I am." Her voice was even, almost emotionless.

"Mallory . . ." He reached out to pull her back into the circle of his arms, but she twisted away.

"No, let me finish the story first."

"But, Mallory—"

"Please." She looked at him squarely then and the expression on her face made him feel sick to his stomach.

Dammit to hell and back. Those depths were murkier than he'd thought. A thousand times murkier. And the worst part was even knowing how much Mallory was suffering, he was helpless because there wasn't a thing he could do to make it better. He groaned. "Okay. Finish it."

"We heard Lindsey coming back. She was singing 'Polly-Wolly Doodle' at the top of her lungs. I started to scream, but Cameron put his hand over my mouth and told me I'd better shut up or he'd have to do her too."

She spoke with all the expression of a zombie. "I shut up, just curled up in the dirt like a frightened sow bug.

"He left. I heard Lindsey ask where I was. Cameron said he didn't know for sure, but he thought maybe I'd gone home for lunch. She said yeah, she was getting hungry too. Maybe she'd better go home. Then I heard the mower start up again, so I knew he wasn't coming back.

"I quit crying finally and just lay there in the dirt, watching a spider spin her web in the latticework." She buried her face against her knees. "I didn't want to remember the smell of his sweat or the feel of his hands." Mallory lifted her head, shrugging slightly. "But I did." She swallowed hard. "I still do."

"Mallory . . ." God, he felt useless.

"After a while the clock on the First Christian Church chimed noon. I knew my mother would be mad if I were late, so I straightened my clothes, washed myself off in the ditch, and went home for lunch. Tuna sandwiches, grapes, and lemon Kool-Aid."

"You didn't tell your parents?"

"I was afraid Cameron would go after Lindsey if I said anything." She shook her head. "I never told a soul until tonight. I thought you deserved an explanation because—" She sighed, a hopeless sound. "I can't make love with you, Brody. No matter how much I want to, I just can't."

Brody felt weak, as if he were suffering acute blood loss. Like somebody'd just cut the heart from his chest. "It doesn't have to be that way, Mallory."

She laid a hand on his. "I wish I could believe you. But I know better. You know better. I flinch whenever a man touches me."

"That's not true. I'm touching you now."

"You know the kind of touching I mean."

He knew, the kind that had landed him flat on his back on the entry deck.

"Brody, believe me, it won't work. Thanks to my past, I'm terminally frigid. I wish things could be different, but I know they never will be, and I like you too much to lie to you."

"Maybe if we take it slowly—"

She shook her head. "You're wasting your time, Brody. You deserve better."

Dammit. So did she.

Mallory's appraisal of her own sexuality was way off base. He knew it as well as he knew his own name. Hadn't he felt her response more than once? She just needed a little coaxing and a lot of reassurance. Hell, there was a world of difference between the forcible rape of a child and the gentle seduction of a woman. Eventually she would realize the truth.

Mallory couldn't tell what Brody was thinking. He hadn't said a word in the last five minutes. Sighing softly, she glanced sideways at him, but his face told her nothing. He was probably fighting a losing battle with revulsion. Talk about shooting herself in the foot.

"Are you sure you wouldn't like something to drink?"

"Not tonight." Brody stood up. "I should be going anyway."

Mallory smiled at him uncertainly. "Thanks. Thanks for everything."

"Yeah." Brody nudged her glasses into place. "See you."

She watched him walk to his Jeep. No good-bye kiss. She wasn't sure if that was good or bad. Had he given up on her? Did she want him to give up on her? She closed and locked the door behind him, then leaned against the sturdy oak panels, her arms crossed.

Brody Hunter. She'd never met anyone who made her feel the way he did. If only she weren't such a screwed-up mess.

Sighing, she headed for the bathroom. A shower and then bed, she decided with a yawn. It had been an exhausting day.

The hot water revived her. Wrapping herself in a towel, she wandered into the kitchen. Her emotional purge had left her with a raging case of the munchies. Unfortunately, she hadn't been to the grocery store in a while and there wasn't much to choose from. A bowl of cornflakes maybe? She checked the refrigerator. Only a trickle of milk, so forget that bright idea.

Fruit? All she found were two black bananas. Gingerly, she transferred their pungent corpses to the garbage.

Suddenly she froze at an unaccustomed sound, her fingers clutching the top edge of her towel. What was that noise? Not the purr of the refrigerator or the hum of the freezer. Not the furnace fan. Not the computer.

She scanned the kitchen. Nothing. The sound didn't originate in the living room, either. And it wasn't coming from either of the guest rooms. Which left only one possibility—her bedroom.

She paused outside the door, listening intently. Bingo. The noise, which sounded a bit like static, was definitely coming from behind her bedroom door. But she still didn't have a clue as to its source. Had she left the radio on? The TV?

The hinges squealed a protest as she eased the door open.

Someone's sleeping in my bed. The line from "The Three Bears" popped into her head.

She poked the supine snorer in the ribs. "Evan Corby! What is going on? How did you get in here?"

He snorted and blinked, rubbing the sleep from his eyes before propping himself on his elbows. "Mallory?"

"Who'd you expect? Baby Bear?"

"Baby Bear?" He blinked again and sat up straighter. For once his hair was rumpled, his clothing wrinkled.

"What are you doing here, Evan?"

He brushed a hand back across his hair and the stray locks fell into place as if by magic. "Waiting for you." He checked his watch. "It's after two. Where have you been?"

"Home for the last hour, not that it's any of your business." She frowned. "What are you doing here? Shouldn't you be getting your beauty sleep for the wedding tomorrow?"

"What wedding? Your *sister* . . ." He made it sound like an insult. "Your *sis*-ter suddenly transformed from a completely reasonable human being into a raving lunatic. After you and Hunter left, she flipped out, started throwing things." He grimaced. "Got me right in the chin with an ashtray. Ceramic. Weighed about five pounds."

"I can't believe Lindsey would make a scene like that in public. What did you do to set her off?" Mallory leaned against the doorjamb, folding her arms across her chest.

A slight flush tinged Evan's perfectly chiseled cheekbones. "I was explaining why you'd mistakenly assumed I was having an affair with that Hooterman woman, and in the process I happened to mention the fact that I'd accepted a job with KBRU. At a huge increase in salary, I might add. Silly me, I thought she'd be pleased."

Mallory raised an eyebrow. "She wasn't?"

"She said I was a gutless wonder who was scared of the competition in a bigger market. She said I was more comfortable being a big fish in a little pond. She said I hadn't even considered her preferences. She said what about *her* professional advancement? I said, 'What profession? You buy underwear for a department store. That's not exactly brain surgery.' And then she threw the ashtray and said the wedding was off."

What an idiot, Mallory thought. He'd probably had this grand career move in the works for months now, but he hadn't bothered to tell Lindsey. In fact, if he hadn't been forced into it, he probably would have saved his news for the honeymoon. *By the way, darling, call the movers as soon as we get back to Portland. Did I mention that we're moving back to Brunswick? What's that? You say you prefer Portland? You say you enjoy your job? But honey, this is a once-in-a-lifetime opportunity. You don't expect me to turn down a dream job just because you have an unhealthy addiction to the Clackamas Mall. Be reasonable.*

She curled her lip in disgust. "Where's Lindsey now?"

He hung his head. "I don't know. She took off in the Lexus, so I borrowed your mother's car and went looking for her. I was hoping she'd come here."

"Here?"

"She always comes running to her big sister when she's upset."

"Think back on the evening, Evan. She was royally ticked off with me even before she got mad at you. Under the circumstances, I don't think she's going to come to me for comfort."

"Oh, right. I forgot." Evan shoved aside the afghan he'd been sleeping beneath and stood up. He hadn't bothered to remove his shoes, she noticed. She eyed the quilt, searching for traces of dirt.

Evan tucked his shirt in, straightened his tie, shrugged into the jacket he'd hung over the ladder-back chair next to the window, then shot a disapproving look her direction. "You know, you really ought to get dressed. It's chilly in here."

She'd forgotten she was standing there in nothing but a towel. But dammit, this was her house, not his. She'd run around buck naked if she wanted to.

"I waited across the street in the car until I froze out. Luckily, I remembered that key you leave under the flowerpot."

Luckily. Oh, yeah. She was definitely going to have to move that key.

"What took you so long getting home?" Had he always been such a whiner?

"Brody and I took the scenic route." She frowned. "Look, Evan, it's late and I'm tired. Why don't you go back to Mother and Daddy's? I'm sure Linz has cooled off by now."

"I don't think so. She was really steamed. She said she didn't want to see me again. Ever."

"Then get yourself a motel room."

"I left my wallet in my other suit."

"Then go wake up a friend. You can't stay here."

"Why not?"

"Because it's my house, and I don't want you here." She turned and marched into the living room. Maybe if she could lure him out on the deck somehow, then slam and lock the door behind him . . .

Evan trotted behind her like a faithful dog. "Mallory, please. For old times' sake. You owe me."

"I *what?*" She whirled to face him, her hands planted firmly on her hips. "You want to explain that? How do I owe you? What do I owe you?"

He gave her that poor-whipped-puppy look that had suckered her every time back in the old days. She'd written him term papers because of that look. She'd run umpteen stupid errands because of that look. She'd even battled ring-around-the-collar because of that look. But the old days were history. Ancient history.

"What do I owe you, Evan?" she repeated.

"Six hundred dollars, for starters."

She sucked for air, completely nonplussed. "What are you talking about?"

"Remember the red dress? The beaded designer dress?"

"The one you bought me to wear to the KBRU Christmas gala?"

"Exactly."

She slumped down onto the love seat. "But, Evan, I didn't want that stupid dress in the first place. You're the one who insisted, remember? You're the one who didn't think my black suit was dressy enough. You're the one who wanted to impress the station owner."

"But you're the one who has the dress." Had he always been this big a jerk?

Mallory shot to her feet. "Fine! You want the dress, take it. Then get out of my life." She dashed into the bedroom and ripped the beaded dress from the garment bag where it had hung ever since the KBRU party two years earlier, then rushed headlong back to the living room. "Here!" She tossed the dress in his face. "Now we're even."

Evan looked at her as if she were crazy. "I don't want the damn dress!" he shouted, tossing it in a glittery pile on the floor. "What would I do with a dress? I sure as hell can't wear it myself, and it would hang like a sack on Lindsey."

"Well, I don't want it, either," she yelled back. "If you don't want it, give it to the Salvation Army." She knew she was being unreasonable, but she was furious. If anyone owed anyone around here, it was Evan Corby. Who'd accompanied him to every boring station function for four long years? Who'd taken his dog to the vet? Who'd chosen Christmas and birthday and Mother's and Father's Day gifts for his parents? Who'd baby-sat with his rotten little spoiled-brat nephew? Who'd ironed his stupid underwear, for crying out loud?

Mallory opened her mouth, but before she could share her thoughts, the doorbell rang. She exchanged a look with Evan. Who would be ringing the doorbell at this time of night?

"Lindsey," they chorused, pushing and shoving each other in a slapstick battle to be the first to get the front door open. Mallory won after a strategic application of her elbows, but she reeled backward in surprise when she saw who was really standing on the front deck.

Evan was the first to regain his tongue. "Hunter! What the hell are you doing here?"

Brody's smile was distinctly unpleasant. "Exactly what I was about to ask you, Corby."

"Evan was just leaving," Mallory said.

"Got what he came for, did he?" Brody's gaze wandered from her bare feet, up her legs, and past the terry cloth wrapping her torso to the cleavage the towel didn't quite cover.

Mallory tugged self-consciously at her towel. "It's not the way it looks."

A smile tickled the corners of Brody's mouth. "No, I guess not, seeing as Corby here still has his tie on."

"Evan didn't come to see me. He was looking for Lindsey. They had a fight."

"A disagreement," Evan said. "A misunderstanding really." He looked down his nose at Brody. "Not that any of this family business concerns Mr. Hunter."

Brody moved her aside and strolled in like he owned the place. Evan, she noticed, took a couple of steps back. Great, she thought, now I have two of them. "Come right on in, Brody. Join the party. I always entertain at two in the morning while I'm dressed in a towel."

"What are you doing here in the middle of the night?" Evan demanded, as if he were her guardian.

"Maybe he was invited over," Mallory said. "Unlike you." She eyed Evan from between narrowed lids. Swear to God, if he did take the job at KBRU, she'd never watch that channel again—except for Saturday-afternoon reruns of *Magnum*. Disgusted, she plopped down on one end of the sofa.

Brody perched on an arm of the love seat. Evan edged toward the door, his eyes shifting nervously from

Brody to Mallory, then back again to Brody. "You didn't answer my question."

"Sorry." Brody raised an eyebrow. "Did you say something?"

Evan's face turned brick red. "I said what the hell are you doing here at this time of night?" He spoke slowly, enunciating each word.

Mallory waved her arm in the air like an overeager student. "No, actually, what you said before was 'What are you doing here in the middle of the night?' "

Evan swore in frustration.

Brody raised both eyebrows this time. "Now, that's not a very nice way to talk in front of a lady."

Evan lifted the corner of his lip in a sneer. "Well, if she invited a sleazebag like you to spend the night, then she's not much of a lady, is she?"

"Get out, Evan!" Mallory jumped up, grabbed the beaded dress from the floor, and threw it at him again. "Take your stupid dress with you too."

Brody shoved himself to his feet and advanced on Evan with athletic grace. "Sleazebag?"

Evan shrank away, holding the sparkly red dress in front of him like a shield. He backed into the door with an audible thunk.

Mallory didn't blame him. The look on Brody's face boded ill for Evan's bridgework.

"I was just leaving." Evan's voice rose a full octave in terror as Brody shoved him out the door.

"And don't come back," Brody growled, slamming the door shut with more energy than was strictly necessary. He turned to face Mallory, and a grin spread slowly across his features. "I really, really like that towel."

She knew her face must reflect her bewilderment. He

liked her towel? It was perfectly ordinary blue terry cloth, the nap of the fabric a little thin in places now; she'd had it ever since college.

Brody's smile grew broader yet.

She glanced down, following his gaze. "Whoops!" She hiked her towel back up to a G-rated position and tucked the overlapping end securely into the top edge. "Why did you come back, Brody?"

"Forgot something."

"What? Your lucky penny?" she asked sarcastically, remembering the line he'd fed her mother.

"Nope."

She caught her lower lip between her teeth. He watched her steadily, the hint of a smile hovering at the corners of his mouth. "Then what?"

Brody sauntered over, never lifting his gaze from hers. "This." He framed her face with his hands, and she felt herself flushing as his touch sparked a response. He slowly bent forward, his gaze still locked on hers, and she vibrated with anticipation.

He's going to kiss me, she thought, surprised by her own lack of panic. *And this time I'm not scared. I'm not scared of Brody at all. I want him to kiss me. I want to kiss him back.*

The touch of his lips still came as a surprise.

Mallory jerked away, not motivated by fear or revulsion, simply startled by the fierce, almost painful emotional jolt. My God, if a mere brush of the lips could set her heart racing and turn her knees to overcooked spaghetti, what would happen if he touched her, really touched her? Another inexplicable case of spontaneous human combustion?

"I've been thinking about your problem." Brody's

voice was a raspy whisper that tickled her mouth and worried her ragged nerves.

She closed her eyes, unable to bear the loving tenderness of his steady gaze. "I have, too, and I'm sorry, Brody. It's not going to work between us."

He kissed her again, gently, with a sweetness that lulled her senses and warmed her heart. "I would never hurt you. You know that, don't you?"

"Yes, but—" He stifled her protest with a kiss so potent that her senses spun in a dizzy vortex. She was Alice, plunging down the rabbit hole. Dorothy, caught in the cyclone. She couldn't breathe; she couldn't think.

Panicking, she pulled away. "I can't do this. It's not that I don't want to. I just can't."

"You don't have to do anything you don't want to do, Mallory." Brody wrapped his arms around her, holding her close, so close she could hear the pounding of his heart.

The problem was she didn't know what she wanted to do. Her mind screamed caution, but her body throbbed everywhere it made contact with his. Mallory moaned in sheer frustration. She wanted him but knew she couldn't have him. Prolonging the agony wasn't fair to either one of them. She pulled away, clutching at her towel.

Brody's smiled a crooked little half smile. "I was afraid of that," he said.

She shook her head sadly. "I'm sorry. I just can't."

He gripped her shoulders and spoke in a low, urgent voice. "That pig forced himself on you when you were a child. You were his victim then, and there was nothing you could do about it. But there's a hell of a difference between being raped and making love with someone who cares for you. You're grown up now, Mallory. You control your destiny. You decide what you want to do. It's okay to say no as long as it's what you really want. But I'm not convinced it is. Think about it, honey. Are you going to avoid sex permanently? He made you a victim once. Don't let him make you a victim for the rest of your life."

Her eyes filled with tears.

Brody watched her face for a moment, then slowly released her. "I'll see you tomorrow," he said.

"Tomorrow," she echoed. She should have been relieved that he'd given in so easily, but all she felt was confusion.

TEN

"Lovely reception. Your father must have dropped a bundle." Great-aunt Bethiah, resplendent in pearls and a peach satin turban trimmed with dyed-to-match chicken feathers, had descended on Mallory the second Brody went off in search of the men's room. "By the way, who's your new young man, dear?"

"His name is Brody Hunter. He's a cop," she added, figuring that was the next question on Great-aunt Bethiah's list.

"Really, dear? What a waste of raw material. Tell him he should move to Hollywood. He could make his fortune there. He's every bit as good-looking as the men on my soaps and better built than any of them."

"Thanks. I'll be sure to pass along your advice."

When a stout female in flowered silk, support hose, and jogging shoes approached, momentarily distracting her great-aunt, Mallory slipped away. Snippets of conversations reached her ears as she wove through the tightly packed bodies.

". . . heard the wedding was almost canceled, but they seem to have patched up their differences . . ."

". . . damn burglars took everything but the kitchen sink . . ."

". . . lovely wedding, beautiful bride . . ."

She paused near the buffet table and stood on tiptoes, scanning the crowd for Brody. He was nowhere to be seen, though she did catch a glimpse of Kyle's lanky form propped against a pillar near the dance floor.

Spotting her, he gave a wave. "Come on over," he mouthed. Despite the seething river of people that separated them, joining Kyle sounded like a wiser course of action than waiting around for Great-aunt Bethiah to pounce again.

Like a salmon struggling upstream against the current, Mallory plunged into the throng, fighting her way through the mass of humanity. Her progress was slow. She had to stop every step or two to greet people she knew. Most remarked on how well she was looking, sounding surprised. At least half a dozen were more direct, bluntly stating how shocked they'd been to hear her sister had stolen her boyfriend.

She coped by gluing a phony smile on her face and saying over and over what a great couple Lindsey and Evan made and hadn't it been a beautiful ceremony?

Kyle's welcoming smile was a beacon. Determinedly, she waded toward him through the swirling currents of social purgatory. "Thanks," she said as he pulled her into a calm eddy near the pillar.

"You remember Tim?" Kyle nodded toward his companion.

"Sure, but I thought . . ." She'd thought he'd made up with Dolph.

"Dolph canceled at the last minute," Kyle explained. "A sudden emergency."

Tim smirked. "Yeah, like maybe a bad hair day."

Kyle ignored the other man's comment. "And Tim was free."

Mallory shook Tim's hand. His skin was slick and smooth, almost as if he were wearing latex gloves. She withdrew her fingers as quickly as possible, doing her best to suppress a shudder.

The bartender looked pretty pleased with himself. "My day off. Perfect timing, no?"

"Perfect." Had Tim somehow engineered Dolph's cancellation? Mallory wondered. She didn't trust him an inch.

"So this is where you disappeared to." Brody slid an arm around her waist, and her heart nearly beat its way past her rib cage.

She hid her shaking hands in the silken folds of her dress. "My move was in the nature of a strategic retreat. My great-aunt Bethiah launched a frontal assault."

The corner of his mouth twitched. "She sounds formidable. Guess I haven't met her yet."

Kyle rolled his eyes. "If you had, you'd remember. Eightyish. Six feet tall, wearing a turban and enough pearls to decorate a Christmas tree."

"Faux pearls," Tim corrected him. "And cheesy ones at that. I'm something of an expert."

Not to mention something of a jerk, Mallory thought.

"Good to see you made it, Brody," Kyle said, offering his hand. "You must be run ragged with all these burglaries we've had lately."

"Not to mention GI Joe. Any leads?" Tim asked.

Brody looked grim. "Damn few."

Tim lowered his voice to a confidential level. "I heard another woman was assaulted last week."

Mallory suppressed a shudder, and Brody pulled her closer in a protective gesture. "Right in her own home, just like the other victims."

"As much publicity as there's been, you'd think people would keep their doors and windows locked." Tim was obviously angling for an insider's view, but Mallory didn't want to hear the gory details. She tried her best not to think about GI Joe if she could help it.

"Not to change the subject, but I read in the paper that you have a lead on the burglaries," Kyle said.

"Yes, we finally discovered the common link, thanks to Mallory. All the home owners were regular Dairy-Best customers who put a hold on their deliveries while they went out of town."

"So the burglar is the ice-cream man?" Tim's bright brown eyes and twitching nose reminded her of an inquisitive hamster.

Brody's expression was noncommittal. "There appears to be a connection with Dairy-Best. Unfortunately, their office is closed on weekends and the manager is out of town, so we won't be able to check employee records until Monday."

Kyle frowned. "Seems like it would have been smarter not to release the information to the paper. Won't this tip off the burglars? I mean, if it were me and I read in the paper that the police were about to crack the case wide open, I'd get the hell out of Dodge."

"Someone leaked the information." Brody's arm tightened around her.

"Hey, not me," Mallory said.

He looked at her, his expression serious. "I thought maybe you'd said something to a friend."

She frowned. "No way. The leak must be in the department."

"You know," Tim said, "I have my own theory about our recent crime wave. I bet one of those right-wing militia groups is responsible. The robberies support the organization and the rapes are the troops' way of letting off steam."

Kyle raised an eyebrow. "I wasn't aware that we had any militia groups in the area."

"We don't," Brody said.

Kyle frowned. "Besides, robbery and rape are two entirely different crimes. I don't see the connection."

"Interesting theory, though," Brody said politely, then turned to Mallory. "Want to dance?"

"Love to," she meant to say, but never got past the first syllable. The heated look in Brody's eyes literally took her breath away. She stiffened instinctively, but he swept her onto the dance floor before her flight reflex could kick in.

"It's okay." His voice, soft and soothing, reassured her. She closed her eyes against a rush of emotion and gradually, one by one, her muscles relaxed.

The band was playing "Dust in the Wind," a song so sad, it normally brought an ache to her chest. This time she was too busy dealing with the unfamiliar sensations flooding her body to pay attention to the bittersweet lyrics. Though her muscles were relaxed, her nerves were on fire.

Her body burned everywhere it made contact with Brody's, her lower back where his hands rested, her front from shoulder to knees where he held her pressed against him, her cheek pillowed against his chest.

"Haven't danced in a while. Hope your feet survive."

So far her feet had no complaints, though other portions of her anatomy throbbed almost painfully in time with the music. She nestled closer, and Brody's scent filled her nostrils, soap and clean, warm male body creating a surprisingly seductive mixture.

Suddenly, unexpectedly, the throb intensified to hot licking flames that burned her from the inside out. Mallory wanted to feel Brody's mouth on hers, to taste his lips.

Are you nuts? the rational part of her brain demanded. *Don't you remember where feelings like that lead?*

Bits and pieces of long-suppressed memories flooded her mind: the sound of her own gasping sobs, Cameron's weight crushing her into the dirt, the odors of sweat and Coppertone, dust and *Cameron* clogging her nose. She stiffened in remembered pain, clamping down hard on her emotions.

Dammit. What had tripped Mallory's alarm this time? She'd been soft and fluid in his arms only seconds ago. Now she was tense again, her muscles taut and quivering. Had the talk of GI Joe brought back the old nightmare?

"May I cut in?" Evan stood at his shoulder.

Brody frowned, silently cursing the other man's lousy timing. "It's up to Mallory."

Giving a slight shrug, she moved into Evan's arms.

Brody caught her shoulder and she glanced up at

him, her eyes wide and startled. "I'll be waiting," he said with a smile.

Her answering smile trembled a little at the edges. "Later," she said.

Brody joined Kyle and Tim on the sidelines. "How long has she known the truth?" Kyle asked.

"Practically from the beginning."

Tim cocked his head to one side. "The truth about what?"

"That I'm not really gay," Brody said.

Tim's eyes opened wide. "Why on earth would she have thought that?"

No one answered his question. Brody watched Mallory swirling around the dance floor in Corby's arms. Was it really necessary for him to hold her quite that close?

Kyle shot Brody an assessing look. "And she didn't call off the date? Maybe I misjudged her."

"I hope so." Brody grinned.

But Kyle's expression was dead serious. "Watch your step, Hunter. Don't hurt her," he said softly, before dragging Tim off to the buffet line.

Brody stared after them in surprise. Kyle Brewster, mild-mannered Kyle Brewster, had just threatened him. Oh, he hadn't come right out and said, "Hurt her and you're dog meat!" but Brody knew what he meant. And he wasn't sure whether to laugh or feel insulted.

Shaking his head in dismay, he propped himself against the wall, where he had an unrestricted view of Mallory and the groom. After watching them for a few minutes, he came to a couple of surprising conclusions. First, Corby might look like Mr. Suave and Sophisticated, but he couldn't dance for beans. And second, the man was an idiot. He must be. How else could you explain his dumping Mallory?

"She's really okay with this, isn't she?"

"What?" He turned to find the bride standing at his elbow.

"Mallory." Lindsey seemed surprised. "She's not the least bit upset about my marrying Evan, is she?"

As they watched, Mallory stifled a yawn.

Brody caught her eye, winking encouragingly. An impish grin lit her face, and she winked back.

Lindsey smiled and waved. "She told me his defection had only bruised her ego, not her heart, but I didn't believe her then. Only seeing them together now, I do."

Lindsey's assessment was accurate. If ever Mallory had carried a torch for Corby, the embers were stone cold now. Her face was frozen in a mask of boredom.

That Corby wasn't in love with Mallory was equally obvious. He'd been talking nonstop during the whole dance. Once, Mallory had started to say something, but he'd cut her off after a few words and she hadn't made a second attempt. Engrossed in his monologue, the bozo hadn't even noticed.

"She's in love with you, isn't she?"

"What?" Brody stared at Lindsey in surprise.

"I thought the whole thing was a big put-on at first, you know, just to save face, but she's really hooked. I can tell by the way she looks at you." She studied him solemnly. "How about you? Are you in love with her?"

How the hell was he supposed to respond to something like that? He discarded his first impulse: None of your damn business! A little too blunt. "What gives you that idea?" he said instead.

"You never take your eyes off her."

"Mallory's not exactly hard to look at." He'd thought she was beautiful that first night in the Blue Russian, and since seeing her in a towel, he'd been having some spectacular recurrent fantasies, mostly concerned with removing the towel in the most creative possible ways. Probably not the sort of detail to share with her sister, though.

"You think she's pretty?"

Brody turned to Lindsey with a smile. "No, I think she's gorgeous. Which is hardly surprising since good looks obviously run in your family."

She batted her eyelashes like a Southern belle. "Why, thank you, sir."

"You're welcome, though actually, I was thinking of Great-aunt Bethiah."

He'd half expected her to pout, but she chuckled instead, and he caught a glimpse of Mallory in her expression.

"Champagne?" Brody snagged a couple of glasses from a passing waiter. "Here." He pressed one of the plastic flutes into her hands and clinked his glass with hers. "To happily ever after."

"Happily ever after it is."

She eyed him closely over the rim of her wineglass. "Actually, I had an ulterior motive in approaching you. There's something I think you ought to know, but I don't know exactly how to put it."

Uh-oh.

"Mallory," she started, then stopped. "This is a lot more embarrassing than I expected it to be."

"Why?"

She flushed. "Because you're not the jerk I thought you were." She gulped down more of her champagne, then said in a rush, "Last night I was furious with Mallory for causing that scene. Then I realized she'd only been trying to protect me. So now I guess it's my turn."

"To make a scene?"

Lindsey uttered a trill of nervous laughter. "I sincerely hope not." She traded her empty glass for a full one and took a quick sip. "I love my sister, and I don't want to see her hurt. She has no defenses against a man like you."

"A man like me?" Brody told himself the knot in his gut was heartburn.

"Single, with every intention of staying that way." Lindsey took another quick sip. "Mallory's not some disposable bimbo, you know. You can't just toss her aside like a piece of trash when you're done with her." She uttered the words with a passionate intensity. Tears trembled on her eyelashes.

Brody spoke softly. "What makes you think I'd do that?"

Lindsey took another sip of champagne before answering. "That's just it. I don't know what you're capable of. I don't really know you, and I don't think Mallory does, either."

Two hours and three glasses of champagne later, Mallory decided she enjoyed dancing with Brody, especially slow dancing. She sighed, snuggling against him. "Is it hot in here?"

"It's warming up." Brody brushed his lips across her forehead and she shivered in reaction. "You ready to go?"

"Almost." She grinned up at him. He looked a little

fuzzy around the edges. She wasn't sure if her contacts had slipped awry or if the champagne was getting to her. "I'll meet you at the door. There's something I have to do."

"Okay. Two minutes. Main entrance. Right under the elk horns."

"Two minutes. Elk horns," she repeated obediently. Then she slipped away to the kitchen, where the extra champagne was chilling in the big commercial cooler. She snagged a bottle, hid it in the folds of her mohair stole, and trotted quickly toward the main door, grinning to herself.

"Where do you think you're going with that champagne, young lady?"

"Daddy!" Mallory almost lost her grip on the bottle.

"I paid top dollar for that damned carbonated French vinegar." Mike Scott sounded fierce enough, but his eyes were sparkling with suppressed laughter. "You and that new boyfriend of yours planning to party all night?"

"Maybe." She grinned. "We haven't discussed it."

Her father patted her shoulder. "It's good to see you having fun for a change, baby. You're way too serious most of the time."

"Not much to laugh about most of the time."

"Oh, Mallory." He pulled her into a hug. "I know I don't say it often enough, but I love you, baby. And somehow, I can't help but feel that this should be your reception that's sending me to the poorhouse, not your sister's."

Mallory leaned back so she could make eye contact. "Me marry Evan? Never would have happened. Believe me, he and Lindsey are much better suited than he and I ever were."

Her father studied her face carefully. "You're sure?" She patted his cheek. "Positive."

A smile crinkled the corners of his eyes. "Good. Glad we got that straightened out." He gave her a quick squeeze, then released her altogether. "Here comes your date with yet another bottle of my overpriced champagne. Apparently the two of you have a lot in common—like a streak of larceny a mile wide. You watch out for that French stuff. It'll sneak up on you."

Laughing, Mallory crossed her heart. "I'll be careful." She turned to Brody with a grin, holding her bottle up so he could see it. "Looks like we both had the same idea."

Brody raised an eyebrow. "At least one of the same ideas. We'll have to see how well the others mesh."

They walked out of the Elks Lodge arm in arm, she teetering a little in her high heels as they crossed the loose gravel of the parking lot. Mallory couldn't remember the last time she'd felt this carefree. Never? If her present euphoria was merely the product of the champagne, then maybe she'd have to add the bubbly stuff to her list of comfort foods. Somewhere between chocolate-covered macadamia nuts and cherry cheesecake.

Brody decided he liked Mallory's playful side. Tugging on the end of his tie, she dragged him into the kitchen. "The glasses are in the cupboard next to the sink. Help yourself. I'm going to go change into something more comfortable, if you don't mind?"

"Not a bit." Smiling to himself in anticipation, he

wondered what she planned to surprise him with. He supposed a towel was too much to hope for. But maybe, just maybe, she'd put on something soft and silky. A negligee? A chemise?

Brody held the opened champagne bottle against his hot forehead for a second or two, then poured the sparkling wine into a couple of stemmed glasses he dug out of the cupboard.

Back in the living room, he set the bottle and glasses on the trunk. He stripped off his tie and tossed it and his suit jacket over the end of the sofa, then made himself comfortable on one end of the love seat.

Okay. Champagne and a love seat. Good so far. But not quite right, either. He studied the room, his head tipped to one side. What's wrong with this picture? he asked himself.

Too much light, he decided. Way too much light. He flicked off the chandelier and two of the three table lamps, then sat back down. Better, but not perfect.

"Why don't you put on a CD, Brody?" Mallory's muffled voice floated out from the back of the house.

He was momentarily distracted by the thought of Mallory in her underwear. She must be down to the underwear by now, probably a lacy bra and a pair of bikini panties. Black. No, red. No, white and semitransparent.

Oh, hell. *Concentrate on something else, moron.* Like, for example, what she'd just said.

Eventually the sense of her words penetrated his brain. CDs. Of course. That was it. That's what was missing. Mood music. "Where do you keep them?" he called.

"In the TV stand. They're right next to the video-tapes."

Brody pulled everything out of the cupboard under the VCR, just in case he'd missed something the first time. He hadn't, unfortunately. The woman had very strange taste in music. He considered his choices—Queen, The Beach Boys, Bette Midler, or Weird Al Yankovic. Not quite what he had in mind. Finally he resorted to eenie, meenie, minie, moe and ended up with Queen—at least after a wee bit of cheating. He'd actually landed on Weird Al the first time, but there was no way he was going to try to seduce Mallory with some guy playing the accordion in the background.

"Where's the CD player?" he called.

"Don't have one," she yelled back.

"What?" he asked, certain he'd misunderstood her.

"I don't have one. Just throw it in the computer."

In the computer? What the hell was she talking about *in* the computer? "What do you mean '*in* the computer'?"

"It's got a CD-ROM."

"Yeah?"

"Never mind. I'll do it." Mallory spoke from behind him.

He turned. Something comfortable. He should have known better than to pin his hopes on the towel. And Mallory really wasn't the Frederick's of Hollywood type. What she was, apparently, was the sweats-and-cow-slippers type.

Well, duh, pea brain, scoffed the logical portion of his brain, *she doesn't know you're planning to seduce her*. Or maybe she did. Maybe the sweats and cow slippers were supposed to be a turnoff. They weren't working, though, possibly because of the way the soft cotton outlined her curves.

Mallory grinned at him, shoving her glasses back up to the bridge of her nose. "Boy, it feels good to ditch the contacts and to get out of those panty hose! Here. Move over." She maneuvered him out of her way with a bump of her hip, pushed a couple magic buttons, and soon Freddie Mercury's voice was blasting from the speakers at a decibel level that rivaled the Concorde.

She played with the mouse a little, adjusting the volume, a wise move in Brody's opinion, since "Bohemian Rhapsody" was the second track and he valued his hearing.

"I poured you some champagne." He indicated the glasses on the trunk.

"That was sweet. Thanks." Mallory retrieved one of the glasses and curled up in the big overstuffed armchair.

Big, but not, he estimated, big enough for two. He settled on the love seat instead.

She yawned. "Whoa! I am whipped! What a day." She shook her head. "Lindsey was a beautiful bride, though, wasn't she?"

"Beautiful," he agreed. Though not, in his humble opinion, as beautiful as her older sister. Even in those god-awful sweats, you could tell Mallory had a chest. And hips. Nicely rounded hips. By contrast, her sister was flat as a board. Not to mention that plastic-coated hair.

Mallory's hair was soft. Like her eyes. And her skin. Especially her skin.

Stop doing this to yourself, diphead. The pads of his fingers itched at the thought of touching that soft, soft skin. He drained his glass, then refilled it. "Want some?" He tipped the bottle toward Mallory.

"Thanks." She smiled at him, looking so sweet and innocent, he felt like a heel.

Dammit, what was he doing? She'd already had too much to drink, and he knew it. Under the circumstances, it would hardly be ethical to seduce her. He was going to have to leave, and the sooner the better.

Ignoring his conscience, Brody sauntered over and perched casually on the arm of her chair. He topped off her glass, then set the bottle on a nearby table.

"This calls for a toast." Mallory lifted her glass. "To Kyle, for finding me a drop-dead-gorgeous hunk."

"To Kyle." Their gazes locked above the clinking champagne glasses. The moment hung suspended in time, an instant of awareness so fragile, Brody was afraid to move, afraid to breathe.

"Brody?" Mallory's mouth looked so soft, so kissable, so close.

What the hell, he thought. One kiss.

But before he could follow through on his intention, Mallory reached up, pulled his face down to hers, and pressed her mouth to his for a brief moment.

"Well, I'll be damned." Brody whispered the words against Mallory's lips, lips that were every bit as soft as they looked. They tasted of champagne.

Mallory made a funny little noise in her throat, halfway between a gasp and a sigh. Her eyes grew large and her glasses slid down her nose in slow motion. "Wow."

Brody grinned. "Double wow." He nudged her glasses back up to the bridge of her nose.

She frowned at him. "I like you, Brody Hunter."

"I like you too."

"I'm glad." She took a deep breath, inadvertently drawing his attention to her chest.

She wasn't wearing a bra. He'd bet a hundred bucks on it.

"I like you," Mallory repeated. "A lot."

"That works out pretty well then, because I like you a lot."

She sat up a little straighter.

Definitely no bra.

"So. Brody. What do you want to do now?"

The answer to that one would probably scare the hell out of her. He grinned. "I'm open to suggestions."

Another deep breath. "We could always make love."

Damn. Brody couldn't have been any more surprised if she'd pulled out a double-barreled shotgun and let him have it right between the eyes. Of course, he'd had three glasses of champagne himself. Maybe his ears were playing tricks on him. "What did you say?"

"You heard me."

"You've had too much to drink, Mallory. The alcohol—"

"I'm not drunk, if that's what's worrying you." She tugged on her earlobe. "No tingle there, even though the rest of me feels like it's burning up."

Brody couldn't keep his eyes off her breasts, the nipples clearly outlined against the soft, thin fleece. Damn. It must be the alcohol talking, whether she believed it or not. He had to get out of here before he did something he'd regret.

ELEVEN

Brody stood up. "I think I'd better go."

"Why?" Mallory pushed herself to her feet, and Brody caught himself staring at her Oregon State sweatshirt. One taut nipple bull's-eyed the *O*.

Tearing his gaze away, he gathered up his tie and suit jacket. "Because." Because if he stayed, he knew he couldn't keep his hands off her.

"That's no answer." She grabbed his arm. "Look at me."

He did. A major mistake. Her glasses were slipping again. He reached out to nudge them back up, but she stopped him.

"No," Mallory said. She took her glasses off and set them on the trunk.

"Why did you do that?"

She smiled. "You're a bright boy. Figure it out." Then she planted a hand in the center of his chest and shoved him backward onto the love seat.

He gave a grunt of surprise as she landed on top of him. "Mallory, what—"

"I've been thinking about what you said."

"I say a lot of things. Refresh my memory."

" 'He made you a victim once. Don't let him make you a victim for the rest of your life.' " Her smile wobbled, then steadied. "I decided not to be a victim anymore. It's time to get on with my life."

His gaze locked on hers for a long, silent moment. "Are you sure?"

She nodded. "All I could think about the whole time we were dancing this evening was how much I wanted to jump your bones."

"I'm shocked," he said, though turned on was closer to the truth.

She smiled, and Brody's heart thumped a slow, erratic rhythm. They kissed, and waves of heat enveloped him.

She licked along the seam of his lips with the tip of her tongue, teasing his mouth open. The taste of her, sweet and hot, drove his blood pressure through the roof.

Ah, depths. Deep, dark, unsuspected depths. This woman was full of surprises.

Just when Brody was sure his lungs were on the verge of collapse, she broke away. "Hot," she gasped, and sat up, rocking against his erection.

Oh, hell. Brody groaned, positive he was going to explode. And it didn't help his condition a bit when Mallory peeled off her sweatshirt.

He'd been wrong. She was wearing a bra after all, a wisp of black lace that revealed more than it covered.

And then it was gone, too, leaving her beautiful breasts free and unfettered.

Surprise held him captive as her sweatpants and cow slippers went flying, followed by a pair of black lace panties.

"Aren't you hot, Brody?" Mallory unbuttoned his shirt and slid her hands inside.

Burning up, he thought, and reached for her, half-afraid she'd stiffen or pull away. Instead, she relaxed into him with a sigh.

Her breasts filled his hands with warmth, and when he brushed his thumbs across her swollen nipples, she moaned and sank her nails in his shoulders.

In a fever of urgency, he sought her mouth again. Her lips seared his, melting the last of his doubts. Mallory wanted him as much as he wanted her.

No time for gentleness now, just a desperate hunger. Without breaking the kiss, he tugged his shirt off and tossed it over the end of the sofa while Mallory fought his belt and zipper.

Together they removed the rest of his clothes in a wild melee of groping hands and twisting legs, and somehow in the struggle, they both ended up on the floor.

Shuddering uncontrollably, Mallory fought her panic. *He's not hurting you*, she told herself. And he wasn't, just nuzzling her neck while supporting most of his weight on his elbows. But she still felt trapped beneath him, as if she'd be crushed at any moment. He was so big, his bare chest broad and muscular, even broader and more muscular than . . .

He raised his head to kiss her again, but she held him off. Squeezing her eyes shut, she tried to block out the pictures in her mind. "No," she begged. "Please, no!"

He froze, and all she could hear was the ragged sound of her own breathing.

"Mallory?" His voice was a husky whisper.

She opened her eyes. Brody's face. Not Cameron's. Brody's. His expression made her heart flutter madly. There was tenderness in the curve of his mouth, caring in his clear, silvery eyes.

"What's wrong?" he asked.

Still shivering, she wriggled out from under him. "I had a flashback."

"But why? What triggered it?"

She shrugged helplessly. "I don't know. All of a sudden I couldn't breathe."

He brushed the hair back off her forehead. "If I do something you don't like, say so and I'll stop. I'm not Cameron. I'm not going to force anything on you. That's a promise." He kissed the tip of her nose, then both eyelids in turn. "Okay?"

"Okay," she whispered unsteadily.

"You're beautiful, Mallory."

She closed her eyes, mesmerized by the sound of his voice.

Rolling back on top, he drew his thumb across her cheekbone, then along the line of her jaw.

"Don't," she said, pulling away.

Brody looked confused for a second. Then his face cleared. "Damn, that's it."

"What?"

"When I'm on top, it triggers your memories."

Was he right? Could it be that simple?

"Honey." His voice was so gentle and full of love, she felt the prickle of tears behind her eyes. "You're supposed to speak up when something bothers you. That was the deal." He kissed her forehead, then rolled her over on top of him. "Better?"

"Yes." She sighed in relief as the claustrophobic feeling ebbed away.

Brody smiled at her, slowly and deliberately, a smile that sent a slow heat burning through her. She was very aware of him, hard against her, aware, too, of the sharp twinges of her own desire. Anticipation of his touch puckered her nipples. *Touch me now*, she thought fiercely.

He cupped her breasts.

Mallory moaned as Brody brushed his thumbs across her nipples with an erotic friction that set her blood on fire. Then tongue and lips and teeth joined his skillful hands to torture her almost past endurance. She squirmed in sheer ecstasy. Could people die of pleasure?

Mallory shut her eyes and gave herself up to sensation. Her body tingled from head to toe. Brody seemed to know exactly how to drive her into a mindless frenzy. She couldn't worry; she couldn't even think. Her existence narrowed to tingling pleasure and throbbing need. She wanted him. She ached for him. "What are you doing to me, Brody?"

"Loving you." He kissed the hollow at the base of her throat, and her heart skipped a beat.

Breathing in shallow gasps interspersed by whimpers of pleasure, she squirmed against him as the delightful sensations grew sharper, their intensity nearing pain. No doubts remained. No fears. She wanted him. "Now, Brody. Please."

"Not yet. Soon." His voice was a gravelly growl that shivered down her spine.

He snaked an arm between their bodies, to find her slick and wet, ready for him. She clenched her muscles at his touch, her shudders exciting him. He frowned fiercely in an effort to master his desire. *Not yet, dammit.* First he had to be sure it was special for her. Mallory deserved special.

He flicked at her, rubbing, teasing until her breathing became even more labored and he could feel her heart thundering wildly in her chest.

Suddenly she jerked, screaming his name and clenching herself around his fingers. He felt the pleasure shudder through her in waves as if it were his own. Finally, she slumped across his chest, sobbing for air. "Oh, Brody. Oh, God. Oh, Brody."

Gently, he turned her over on her back. She was beautiful, her eyes still glazed and unfocused in the aftermath of her orgasm, her mouth pink and swollen from his kisses. And her body . . . God, she was gorgeous. He touched one full breast. She felt so soft against his callused palm, so feminine.

A smile lit her face. "I never dreamed . . . I mean, I thought all that ecstasy stuff was a gimmick dreamed up by romance writers. Why didn't someone tell me?"

"Want to try it again?" Brody trailed a line of kisses down the side of her neck while his hands explored her delectable curves and hollows.

"They say practice makes perfect," she whispered.

Delighted with her response, he moved down her body, drawing the tip of his tongue along the shallow depression in the center of her stomach. He paused to flick her navel, then slid even farther down to the promise of pleasure hidden by tight blonde curls.

She tasted of passion.

Mallory moaned at the first flick of his tongue. In seconds she was writhing beneath him, her hands buried in his hair. "I can't last much longer, Brody." Her words were breathy. "Do you have any protection? I want to feel you inside me this time."

"Oh, yes." He reached for one of the condoms he'd bought the day after he met her. As he adjusted the latex sheath he felt Mallory's gaze on him and turned to look at her.

A smile curved her lips. She ran her hand along the muscles of his thigh. "Kyle promised me drop-dead gorgeous, but he never mentioned sweet or loving or tender."

His heart did a funny little flip-flop in his chest. "You bring out the best in me."

He started to lift her onto him, but she stopped him. "Try it on top," she whispered. "I think it'll be all right now."

He hesitated a second, then covered her body with his own, reassured by the trust he saw in the depths of her eyes.

She spread her legs in welcome and he thrust inside her. A perfect fit. Mallory was where he belonged.

She wrapped her legs around him, pulling him deeper. With a groan, he surrendered to the fierce clamor of their mutual need.

He plunged into her again and again, his pleasure sharpened to a keen edge by the knowledge that they were together this time, Mallory's harsh sighs and ragged breathing as out of control as his own stifled groans and breathless endearments. And just when the pleasure became too intense to endure, the ecstasy too exquisitely painful, he felt Mallory's muscles spasming around him. As she shouted his name he fell off the edge of the world in a shattering climax of his own.

Brody woke up in Mallory's bed with a world-class hard-on and thought for a second he was having another one of those Mallory-in-a-towel dreams when she emerged from the bathroom on a cloud of steam. But then she dropped the towel and curled up beside him, her skin warm and still slightly damp from her shower, and he realized his dream had come true. "I love you," she whispered.

I love you, too. He wanted to say the words. It wasn't a lie. He did love her. But the memory of all his parents' failed marriages stopped him. How many times had they said those words, then lived to regret them? And what made him think he was any different?

Mallory pulled away, studying his face. A slight frown knitted her brow. "Something wrong?"

"No."

She chewed at her lower lip. He could tell she wasn't buying it. "Let me guess. You're one of those I-don't-want-to-talk-it-to-death guys. You just want to roll over and get some sleep."

"No, but if you want to roll over"—he paused, grinning wickedly—"I'd be glad to show you a few new tricks."

Mallory's eyes widened as his words registered. Then she grabbed a pillow and whacked him over the head.

Brody ripped the pillow from her grasp and pinned her to the mattress. "First you try to beat me senseless. What's next on your agenda? Drag my unconscious body out to the Dumpster?"

"All I have is a trash can," Mallory protested, laughing helplessly. "You wouldn't fit."

Brody silenced her with a kiss that started hot and was definitely headed toward meltdown.

The phone rang.

"Ignore it," he muttered against her lips. She tasted so damn good.

"I can't."

"Sure you can. Just concentrate on something else. Here. I'll help." He brushed his knuckles lightly across her nipples.

She shivered in reaction but still pushed him away. "No, Brody. I have to get the telephone." She squinted at the clock on the bedside table. "Nobody calls at six-eighteen on a Sunday morning unless it's important."

"It's probably your sister calling to ask if you know anything about the red beaded dress she found in Corby's suitcase."

Mallory sat up and reached for the phone. "Or Mom wanting me to chauffeur Great-aunt Bethiah to the airport." She made a face, then picked up on the fourth ring. "Hello? Yes. What? Would you mind repeating that?"

"What?" asked Brody.

Frowning in concentration, she shushed him. "Uh-huh. Don't worry. I'll track him down."

"Track who down?" Brody pressed closer in a vain attempt to hear the other side of the conversation.

"Hush." She whacked him again with the pillow.

"No, not you, Kyle," she said into the receiver. "Brody."

"What does Kyle want?"

"If you'd be quiet for two seconds, maybe I could find out." Mallory gave him a look. He knew that look. It was the one teachers used to quell difficult students. He slid one hand up her thigh to remind her he was no student.

She jumped.

He grinned. "I was being quiet. Lasted more than two seconds too."

She wasn't listening. All her attention was on Kyle. Why the hell was Kyle calling anyway? It was practically the middle of the night. Brody didn't mess around with Kyle's love life, so why was Kyle doing his best to screw up Brody's? Brody studied the tense angle of Mallory's shoulders, the tightness at the corners of her mouth, and knew suddenly that Kyle wasn't playing games. Something was wrong.

"We'll be right there," Mallory said, and hung up.

"Right where?" he asked.

"The police station."

Mallory made Brody drive. She was in no condition to be behind the wheel of a car. Upset as she was, she'd probably run them into a power pole.

Brody lifted one hand off the steering wheel, reached across, and gave her shoulder an encouraging squeeze. "Tell me what Kyle said. His exact words, if you can remember them."

"He's under arrest. The cops think he's the one behind the burglaries, thanks to a tip from an anonymous informant. They showed up at Kyle's place with a search warrant and found a pile of stolen merchandise hidden in his carriage house."

"How did Kyle explain being in possession of stolen property?"

"I'm not sure. He didn't say. He was pretty shaken up. But Kyle didn't steal anything, Brody." She spoke earnestly.

"Then how did it get there?"

"I don't know." She was fresh out of bright ideas at the moment, her brain about as useful as a wad of Silly Putty. She let her head fall back against the headrest. God, she was tired. She felt as if she hadn't slept for weeks. "He was framed." Mallory sat up straight. "Yeah, that's it. Somebody must have framed him."

"Why?"

"What do you mean 'why?' And what's with all these questions?" She stared hard at Brody's profile. "You sound like a cop."

The corner of Brody's mouth twitched as if he were trying not to smile. "I am a cop."

"Whose side are you on?" She eyed him suspiciously. Didn't years of friendship count for anything with him? He'd known Kyle for longer than Mallory had. Surely that meant something. He must realize as well as she did that Kyle Brewster didn't have a dishonest bone in his body.

Brody pulled into the big lot next to city hall. He parked in the same space he'd used the last time they'd been here. *Déjà vu all over again.* Something niggled at the edge of Mallory's mind, but she couldn't pin it down.

She hugged her jacket around her, feeling cold. "Whose side are you on?" she asked again.

"Hey!" He kissed the tip of his forefinger, then pressed it against her mouth. "I'm one of the good guys, remember?"

Which didn't really answer her question.

"I want to talk to Kyle Brewster," Mallory said for the third time. She spoke quietly, her temper well in check.

"I'm afraid that's not possible right now." The faded blonde behind the reception desk sounded like a broken record.

"When *will* it be possible?"

The blonde cracked her gum. "Hard to say."

"Okay, then. How about I speak to someone who *can* say? Who's in charge here?"

"Officer Armstrong, but she's busy right now."

Busy grilling Kyle like a trout, she'd bet. "When can I speak to her?"

Blondie shrugged her linebacker shoulders in a gesture that looked more than a little threatening. "When she's not busy, I suppose."

"Logical."

The sarcasm bounced right off the woman's massive chest. She just smiled vaguely, nodded, and went back to the find-a-word puzzle she'd been working before Mallory's approach.

Mallory was so frustrated, she felt like punching someone. Preferably the jerk who had framed her friend, but Officer Regan Armstrong and the blonde behind the counter were near the top of the list too. She'd been hanging around the police station for over an hour now and she still didn't know squat. And to add insult to injury, Brody had disappeared.

He'd left half an hour before, saying he had to make a call, but when she'd checked on him a few minutes ago, he wasn't anywhere near the line of pay phones in the entry and no one out there remembered seeing him.

Damn.

She stared at the frosted clerestory windows high on the east wall. Daylight lightened the room, but her thoughts remained a gloomy midnight black. If everything was on the up-and-up, then why were they giving her this bureaucratic runaround? Where were they keeping Kyle, and what were they doing to him?

She had visions of a bleak, concrete-walled interrogation room. Glaring spotlights. Cattle prods. Okay, maybe no cattle prods, but lots of intimidation, the old good cop/bad cop routine.

"Mallory?"

She jumped a good six inches when Brody touched her shoulder. "What?"

"I have news."

She turned to face him. He looked as rotten as she felt. Dark circles ran halfway down his cheeks, his eyes were bloodshot, and he sported some heavy-duty beard stubble. *No news is good news.* And the corollary to that was . . .

Suddenly she didn't want to hear whatever Brody had to say. "Kyle?"

He nodded.

"They really believe he's behind all the thefts?"

"The evidence is overwhelming." Brody sounded tired.

Her protest was instinctive, immediate. "Overwhelming maybe, but circumstantial. No one saw Kyle steal anything. They couldn't have because he didn't."

"No one's accusing him of theft."

"Then why is he under arrest?"

"To be perfectly accurate," Kyle said from behind her, "I'm out on bail."

"Kyle!" Mallory threw her arms around his neck. "I've been so worried! Nobody would tell me anything." She backed away, holding him at arm's length. "Are you okay? They didn't hurt you, did they?"

"We're not really into police brutality here in Brunswick," Brody said.

"I'm fine," Kyle assured her. He smiled. "Honest."

She studied him suspiciously. Kyle was hiding something. She could tell by the way he kept glancing over at Brody. "You didn't sound fine on the phone."

"Well, I'm out now."

Mallory frowned. He must know how lame that sounded. What was going on? She could feel the undercurrents in the room, threatening to drag them all under.

Kyle cast another quick, almost furtive glance at Brody. Didn't he trust his friend?

She glanced up at Brody herself, but his face told her nothing. He looked worried, but under the circumstances, who wasn't?

Shrugging off her unease, she turned back to Kyle. "I got in touch with your lawyer."

He bobbed his head. "Yeah, I know. He's the one who arranged bail."

"Great. But I'm confused. What did they arrest you for," she asked, "if it wasn't suspicion of robbery?"

"We think he's the fence." Officer Armstrong's voice grated on Mallory's nerves like a rasp.

She swiveled slowly to face the redhead. " 'We' meaning you or 'we' meaning the entire Brunswick police force?"

"Everyone involved in the case agrees." Her stony gaze locked on Kyle. "Don't leave town, Brewster. We'll be keeping an eye on you."

"You can put me under surveillance from now until hell freezes over," Kyle said, "but you won't see anything incriminating because, dammit, like I've been telling you moronic bastards for the last three hours, I'm not guilty."

Kyle must be upset, Mallory thought. She'd never known him to use so much profanity.

A cynical expression settled across Officer Armstrong's face. "Yeah, and I'd be a millionaire if I had a dollar for every time I've heard that one, buddy."

Mallory put one hand on Brody's arm, another on Kyle's. "Come on, guys. Let's get out of here."

"You know, Detective . . ." A nasty, sneering smile bared Regan Armstrong's prominent incisors, yet did nothing to lighten her expression.

Mallory shivered.

". . . a person ought to be careful who he's friends with. When you hang out with the wrong crowd, people start to wonder."

"She's a bitch," said Mallory as soon as they were out in the Jeep. She wasn't any more into profanity than Kyle, but when the epithet fit . . .

"She's a cop," Kyle corrected. "A cop who's convinced I'm guilty."

Brody twisted the key in the ignition, revving the engine more than necessary. "The evidence is pretty damn convincing. Regan wouldn't be much of a cop if she ignored it."

Mallory's voice rose a full octave in disbelief. "Are you two defending that woman?"

Brody slammed the gearshift into reverse, backed up, then took off with a squeal of tires. Mallory nearly bit the tip of her tongue off when he bounced them over the speed bump at the exit.

"Dammit!" Brody swore. "All I said was the evidence was heavily against Kyle. What's Regan supposed to think when she discovers ten thousand dollars' worth of stolen property in Kyle's carriage house? Especially when there's only one key to the damn place and it's hanging on Kyle's key ring. Who has access to your keys, Kyle?"

Brody ran the yellow light at the intersection of Northwest Fourth and Park Boulevard, narrowly missing being hit broadside by a big cattle truck anticipating the green. He swore under his breath.

Mallory gripped the dashboard with both hands. She shot a glance at Kyle in the backseat. He looked miserable.

Brody's mouth was a grim line. "Well, Kyle? Tell her. Tell her who has access to your keys."

Kyle shrugged. "Me. Just me." He closed his eyes for a second, took one deep breath, and slowly exhaled. "But I didn't do anything wrong. I don't know how that stuff got there. I swear."

"I believe you." Mallory's voice was warm with reassurance. "And so does Brody. Good grief, he's known you longer than I have. He certainly ought to know what sort of person you are by now." She thought hard. "Lots of people could have lifted your keys without your knowing—Dolph, for one, or maybe someone at KBRU. Think, Kyle. Did you loan anyone your keys lately?"

Kyle buried his head in his hands. "No one."

Brody squealed the tires again, taking the left turn onto Eighth Street ten miles an hour too fast.

Worry sharpened Mallory's voice. "You're not taking this seriously, are you, Brody? You don't suspect Kyle, do you?"

Brody pulled to a jerky stop in front of Kyle's house. He looked sick. "I don't want to, but the evidence . . ."

"The evidence speaks for itself." Kyle spoke bitterly. "Isn't that what Officer Armstrong kept saying?"

Mallory was so frustrated, she felt like smacking both of them. "Yeah, and it's screaming 'frame-up,' only nobody but me is listening."

Brody leaned his forehead against the steering wheel, not saying anything. Kyle was silent too. They both looked defeated.

Dammit, couldn't they see what was going on? "Someone's framing you, Kyle. I don't know why, but I bet I know who."

"Who?" Both men swiveled in unison to stare at her.

"Officer Armstrong."

Brody tipped his head to look at Mallory. She could tell he liked the idea. "Why, though? Why would Regan Armstrong risk her reputation by framing an innocent man?"

Valid question. Unfortunately, a valid answer didn't spring immediately to mind. She shrugged. "To get even with you?" His expression told her how unlikely that was. "I don't know."

"Right," said Brody. "And that's the problem. Neither do I. Just because you can't stand someone, that doesn't automatically make them one of the bad guys."

"And just because you like someone," Kyle said, "that doesn't automatically make them one of the good guys." He levered himself out of the backseat and onto the sidewalk. "Thanks for the ride." The back door shut with a click of finality.

"Kyle!" she protested, but he ignored her, moving slowly toward his house. She hated the defeated slump of his shoulders, the weary shuffle of his feet. "I'm scared, Brody. I've never seen Kyle this down before. Not even when he was having trouble with Dolph." She clenched her hands together. "We're his friends. We've got to do something."

Brody shifted into first, easing away from the curb. "Like what?"

"Don't ask me 'like what?' You're the detective."

"Only it's not my case."

"Excuse me? You care more about stupid protocol than you do about your friend? This isn't a joke, Brody. He could end up behind bars if somebody doesn't do something."

Brody shook his head. "I'm not saying I can't do anything. I'm just saying it won't be easy, and right now I'm too damn tired to think straight, let alone plan strategy. I need some sleep. I'm on swing today, covering for the sergeant." He glanced at his watch. "If I push it, I can be in bed by ten. That'll give me four hours."

"But, Brody, Kyle might not have four hours. If

someone's gone to all this work to frame him, they're not going to stop now. Next thing you know they'll be 'finding' a stash of cocaine in his flour canister or a dead body in his freezer."

He yawned. "If they do, give me a call."

TWELVE

Though she would have sworn she was too keyed up to rest, Mallory fell asleep slumped in a corner of the love seat shortly after Brody brought her home. She didn't wake up until her mother barged through her unlocked front door a little before six that evening.

"Baby, you look sick!" she said by way of greeting.

Mallory sat up, yawning. "Late night. What brings you over?"

April perched on the edge of the sofa. "Did you know your friend Kyle had been hauled down to the police station for questioning?"

"Yes, but he's out on bail now."

Her mother frowned. "I don't think so. Not so soon. I just heard it on the radio a few minutes ago."

Mallory pulled a throw pillow into her lap, hugging it to her stomach. "Heard what exactly?"

"Your boyfriend was the one who took him in."

"Brody?" Mallory sat up straight, flinging the pillow

aside. "What are you talking about? Brody didn't arrest Kyle. He wouldn't. He couldn't."

April crossed her legs. "I'm just telling you what I heard. According to the radio, police investigators discovered a secret bank account in Kyle's name, and Detective Brody Hunter hauled him in for questioning."

"I don't believe it."

"Turn on the TV and double-check, then." She glanced at her watch. "It's just six now. Time for KBRU's *Evening Report.*"

Mallory grabbed the remote from the top of the trunk and flipped to Channel 5 just as the anchorman launched into his spiel: "Our top story tonight is a shocking one, especially for those of us here at—"

"See? What did I tell you? It's Kyle he's talking about."

Mallory shushed her mother and punched up the volume. Her gut churned acid. Why had she wasted the whole day sleeping when she should have been doing something to help Kyle?

"There! I told you so!" April crowed. She pointed at the screen. Videotaped footage of Brody escorting Kyle into the police station ran to the accompaniment of a brief report. Thanks to her mother's excited commentary, Mallory only caught about half the audio, but the video clip told the whole story.

Hauled in for questioning twice in the same day. Betrayed by a trusted friend. Kyle must be in shock.

Mallory was. "How could he do it?"

"Maybe he needed the money," her mother suggested.

She stared at April in confusion. "What?"

"Maybe Kyle got involved because he needed the

money. You know, like maybe somebody found out he was gay and threatened to tell unless he paid them hush money."

"Mom, Kyle's sexual orientation is no secret. Everybody in town knows he's gay."

"Then who were you talking about?"

"Brody." Mallory sighed heavily. How could he have aligned himself with Regan Armstrong? He must know as well as she did that Kyle wasn't guilty. What was he thinking?

Her mother leaned closer, eyeing her narrowly. "You really don't look good, Mallory. Are you sure you're all right?"

"I'm fine," she lied.

"You're worried about Kyle, aren't you? Fencing stolen property is a serious charge."

"Someone's framing him, Mother."

"But the evidence—"

"Is circumstantial. I'm sure he'll be cleared eventually."

"I hope so. I've always been fond of that boy. Now, if they'd arrested that creepy little man he brought to the wedding, I wouldn't have been a bit surprised."

Tim. Of course. "Mother, you're a genius!"

"I am?"

"Definitely. I think you just solved the case."

Tim. Why hadn't she thought of him before? She knew the Blue Russian was involved in the burglaries. Hadn't she overheard that suggestive conversation between Dimitri Ivanovich and Arlo Junior with her own ears? Working at the Blue Russian didn't prove Tim was involved, of course, but it did mean he had possible access to stolen goods. And he'd had ample opportunity to get at Kyle's keys on several occasions, including last night. Dammit, the little worm had been setting Kyle up from the very beginning. She'd bet on it.

"The lieutenant get anything out of your buddy, Brewster?"

Brody glanced up from his desk, frowning. "What are you doing here, Regan? Aren't you on days?"

"I traded with Andy. It's his anniversary." She leaned against his desk, her expression closer to a sneer than a smile. "Why are *you* here so late, Detective?"

"I'm filling in for Sergeant Ryan."

"Yeah?" She straightened, fussing with her holster, but didn't move away.

What the hell was she up to now? Brody wondered. "Can I do something for you?"

"They release your friend yet?"

He'd ignored her the first time, but she couldn't let it go. *Inquiring minds want to know.* "Yes, he answered the lieutenant's questions, then went home."

She narrowed her eyes. "I guess it pays to have friends in high places."

"Meaning?"

"The guy's under suspicion of fencing half a million dollars' worth of stolen goods. We found ten thou in jewelry, guns, and electronic equipment hidden on his property. Then we get tipped to the fact that he has cash socked away in a secret account. Under normal circumstances, we'd have put the bastard in cuffs and hauled his butt down to the station in a patrol car." She smiled unpleasantly. "No cuffs for your pal, plus he gets escorted in by a plainclothes detective. *You*, his buddy. No lights. No siren. Nothing."

"Still made the six-o'clock news, I noticed. Are you the one who called the television crew?"

She didn't say a word, but her self-satisfied smirk was answer enough.

"Being identified on TV as a cop is going to limit my effectiveness in undercover operations. Ever think of that?"

Her smirk grew wider. "Kinda like being neutered, huh?" She turned and sauntered out of the station, chuckling to herself.

Brody rolled his shoulders, trying to loosen the knotted muscles. Armstrong was a manipulative bitch, but he was a damn fool to let her get to him.

He studied the numbers in the bankbook the informant had given him. Kyle might not be languishing downstairs in lockup, but he was still in serious trouble. Numbers don't lie, he told himself wearily. But people did.

Mallory stared blankly at the flickering television screen, trying to sort out her jumbled thoughts. Kyle was in big trouble. That much was clear. Clear, too, was the fact that Brody wasn't going to be the one to help him. By taking Kyle into custody, he'd announced his allegiance to the enemy camp.

Regan Armstrong. Mallory remembered the redhead's sniping comment to Brody as they'd left the station earlier. *When you hang out with the wrong crowd, people start to wonder.* Was Brody really worried about what other people thought? Or was the issue more complicated than she realized? He was a cop. So maybe he considered dragging Kyle downtown his duty. But duty doesn't justify persecution, she argued to herself. How many Nazi soldiers had told themselves they were just doing their duty? Duty was no excuse.

Mallory pressed a hand to her burning chest, where heartbreak masqueraded as indigestion. A bitter smile curved her lips. What was the prescription for a broken heart anyway? Take two Tums and call me in the morning?

"Dammit, Brody. You don't really think Kyle's involved, do you?" she asked aloud. He knew there was a connection with the Blue Russian, knew Arlo Junior and Dimitri Ivanovich were in it up to their ears. "So why didn't you haul them in for questioning?"

No answer except the inane squawking of the television.

It all came back to Tim. He might look harmless, but she'd bet he was the one who'd planted the stolen items at Kyle's and tricked up a bogus bank account as part of the frame. She shuddered to think what else he might arrange. A phony suicide with a full confession pinned to Kyle's lifeless body? It was the obvious solution. The cops would fall for it, too, and the real crooks would get off scot-free.

Dammit, she couldn't just sit here waiting for the ax to fall. She had to do something to stop this insanity.

Grabbing the phone directory, she located the number for the Blue Russian, then dialed with trembling fingers. One ring. Two. "Pick up," she whispered. "Come on. Pick up." Not that she had a clue what she'd say if she did reach Tim.

On the third ring the machine answered and a recorded version of Dimitri Ivanovich's voice informed her she'd reached the Blue Russian, but that they were closed on Sundays. She hung up in frustration, a frustration that soon edged toward fear. Dammit. Right this minute Tim could be hammering the final nail in Kyle's coffin.

Or maybe not. Kyle was in police custody, she remembered with relief. She still needed to warn him, though.

Hands shaking, heart pounding, she dialed the Brunswick Police Department. Would they even let her talk to Kyle? If not, she decided, she'd ask for Brody and make him listen to her theory, whether he wanted to or not.

Unfortunately, the dispatcher couldn't put her in touch with either man. Kyle had been released already and Brody'd left on his dinner break. "If it's urgent, though, I can page Detective Hunter and have him call you back," the woman offered.

"Thanks." Mallory gave her the number.

Time crawled as she paced the floor, waiting for Brody's call. What was taking him so long? she wondered, then realized barely a minute had passed. She knew she had to be patient, but wasting time when Kyle's life might be in danger went against the grain.

He must be home by now. Instead of waiting around for Brody to get back to her, she should be contacting Kyle, warning him. She grabbed the phone again and dialed Kyle's number only to reach a busy signal.

She slammed the receiver down. Dammit!

Waiting any longer was pointless. Kyle was in danger. She had to do something. Grabbing her car keys, she headed out the door.

———————◆———————

What a miserable night. Icy rain streaked down the windshield and battered against the Jeep's metal roof. Shivering, Brody folded himself behind the wheel and stuck his key in the ignition. His pant legs were soaked from his sprint across the parking lot, and water dripped from his hair down his neck in a steady stream.

Flipping on the heater, he turned onto Northwest Fourth and headed for the strip of fast-food places out by the freeway. He'd been reviewing the evidence against Kyle for the last four hours. If this was a frame, whoever'd arranged it was a damn genius. His stomach twisted in a knot as he considered the alternative—the possibility that his friend was guilty, after all.

Jeez. Dinner break. What a joke. At this rate he'd be better off with a couple of Rolaids and a swig of Pepto.

His beeper went off just as he hit the road construction on Idaho Avenue. Since traffic was heavy, he decided to wait until he was through the bottleneck before checking in. Hell, it was probably just Hawkins with his hourly report from the stakeout.

Brody pulled into the line at Wendy's drive-through, put the Jeep in neutral, and called in on the car phone. He had two messages, the expected one from Hawkins and another from Mallory. Hawkins could wait a couple more minutes, he decided. He dialed Mallory's number. Odd, he thought when her machine answered. Why leave the house when she was expecting his call?

He punched in the number for the station and asked to talk to whichever dispatcher had fielded Mallory's original call. When Laurie Fisher came on the line, he quizzed her, trying not to sound as worried as he felt.

"Did she say why she wanted to talk to me?" he asked for the second time.

"Like I told you before, no. She seemed upset, though. Real jumpy. And come to think of it, she may have had a new lead to report in the Brewster case."

His heart made a lunge for his throat, damn near strangling him. "Why do you say that?"

"Because she asked to speak to him first."

Brody swore.

"Excuse me?" Laurie didn't take any crap from anybody. Not even detectives.

"Sorry," he said. "And thanks. I gotta check in with Hawkins."

The rain was a steady downpour by the time Mallory pulled into Kyle's driveway, and despite her hooded sweatshirt, she was soaked before she hit the porch. Breathing hard from her mad dash to the house, she leaned on the doorbell and tried to think of a tactful way to tell Kyle she suspected his new boyfriend had set him up to take the fall on the fencing charge and might very well be planning to kill him.

"It's about time!" Kyle snapped as he jerked the door open. When he recognized Mallory, he froze, an almost comical look of dismay on his face.

"Kyle?" Mallory said after they'd stared at each other in silence for a slow ten count. "It's pouring. Aren't you going to ask me in?"

His face cleared, and he backed out of the way. "Sure. Come on in. Sorry to sound so cranky. I was expecting a pizza delivery, and the guy's late."

She stepped inside, and he closed the door. She grinned. "Probably related to Brody."

Kyle didn't say a word, but his grim expression spoke volumes.

"He's not your enemy, you know."

Kyle's right eyebrow shot up. "No? Well, with friends like that . . ." Then, as if noticing for the first time that she was dripping all over his polished parquet entry hall, he said, "Let me get you some towels. You're soaked." He headed upstairs at a trot.

Mallory dragged her hood down and tried to fluff her soggy hair but gave it up as a lost cause. Her glasses were blurry—too bad some genius couldn't invent glasses with built-in windshield wipers—but she didn't have anything dry enough to wipe them with. She made do with the tail of her denim shirt, which was only semidamp, having been protected by both a layer of jeans and a layer of sweatshirt. An improvement anyway, she thought as she shoved her glasses back in place.

Kyle came clattering down the stairs two at a time, a stack of towels in his arms. As she turned to take them she noticed the pile of luggage next to the newel post, and her heart fell through the floor. Her mouth went dry. "Planning a trip?"

A rueful smile tilted the corners of Kyle's mouth. "Would you believe me if I told you I was going to visit my sick old auntie? No, I didn't think so."

"You're skipping town, aren't you? It wasn't a frame. You were guilty all along." She took a ragged breath. "Why, Kyle?"

He shrugged. "I needed the extra income. This house is a money pit. It breaks my heart to leave it behind, though I suppose Rio offers a few compensations."

He shoved the towels into her hands. "Strip off your wet things and I'll toss them in the dryer."

"No, thanks. I'm fine as I am."

"Mallory, don't be silly. You're drenched. You'll end up with pneumonia."

"Pneumonia? A bullet? What's the difference?"

"I'm not going to kill you!" Kyle looked so affronted, she almost laughed. "I'm not a murderer."

"And I'm not stupid. You can't afford to let me go. I know too much."

She stiffened at the sound of pounding from the back of the house. "What's that?"

"Pizza's here."

"At the back door?"

"They must have seen your car parked in the driveway. My deliverymen are shy. In fact, it's probably not a good idea for them to see you at all." Taking her arm in an iron grip, Kyle shoved her into the powder room under the stairs. "Don't make a sound. Please. I don't want you to get hurt."

"Too late, my friend." Her eyes filled with tears. "I trusted you. I cared for you."

A shadow of remorse darkened his face. "I'm sorry," he said, and locked her in.

"Hawkins? Detective Hunter here. Got any movement over your way?"

"Big time, Detective."

"Oh, yeah?" The hairs stood up on the back of Brody's neck.

"About ten minutes ago a car drove up. Female gets out and rings the bell. Brewster lets her in."

"A blonde?"

"Couldn't tell. She had her hood pulled up. It's been raining like hell."

"Any sign of her since she went inside?"

"No, but right after she arrived, two guys in a dark-colored minivan eased by dead slow, like they were checking the place out. Parked on the side street and went in through the back gate."

"Descriptions?"

"Gimme a break, Detective. It's pitch-dark and dumping rain besides. All I can tell you is I'm pretty sure they were both males and one of them was huge, about six-eight and bulky enough for the pro wrestling circuit."

Brody swore. Arlo Junior. And the second man was probably Ivanovich. Unless someone else was involved that they didn't know about. "Call for backup. Now. No lights, no sirens. And nobody goes in until I get there."

"What if the suspects take off in the meantime?"

"Follow 'em."

As Brody hung up he realized he wasn't going anywhere in a hurry. He was boxed in, three cars ahead of him, two lined up behind him, all waiting for their turn at the drive-through window. *Hell.* If he had to wait for the damn line to move, he'd be too late for sure. Sweat beaded his forehead; he tasted bile. *Mallory.*

Watching his rearview mirror, he backed up to within inches of the car behind him, hoping the driver would take the hint, but all the guy did was lie on his horn, so Brody went with Plan B. Twisting the steering wheel, he angled the Jeep toward the curb separating the drive-through lane from the parking lot. Then he shifted into four-wheel drive and bounced up and over the barrier without—thankfully—losing his muffler or his tailpipe. He pulled onto the street with a squeal of tires and was doing forty by the time he hit the yellow light at the first intersection.

"Whose car is that in the driveway?" Even muffled by the heavy wooden door that separated them, Mallory recognized the speaker's voice. Dimitri Ivanovich. His accent was a dead giveaway.

"My neighbor's," said Kyle. "Every time it rains, the storm sewer backs up and floods his parking area." His lie was so plausible, she started to wonder how much trust to put in his assurance that he meant her no harm.

"I didn't see no flooded driveway." She knew that voice too. Arlo Junior, the last living Neanderthal. "You trying to pull some kind of double cross, boss?"

"Arlo, shut up." Kyle's voice held just the right degree of irritation. "We don't have time for this. Come Monday morning, the cops are going to access my bank records, looking for confirmation of their suspicions. That's why I'm leaving tonight, before they freeze my assets. If you two are smart, you won't hang around, either. They've already made the connection with Dairy-Best, Arlo. Once they discover you're the Dairy-Best driver . . ."

"I'm not going nowhere without my money," Arlo said.

"Why do you think I called you over here?"

"Actually," Dimitri said, "it occurred to me that you might have cut a deal with the cops. Say, traded us for an easier sentence?"

"I wouldn't do that," Kyle said flatly. "I asked you over so we could split the money."

"What money?" Dimitri asked. "You see any money, Arlo?"

"It's upstairs in my bedroom. Let me go get it."

"I don't think so. Pat him down, Arlo. See if he's wearing a wire."

"Hey, what is this?" Fear put a sharp edge on Kyle's voice. "You can put the gun away, Dimitri."

"I don't think so. Check him, Arlo."

A pause, then she heard Arlo say, "He's clean."

"Why are you two so paranoid?" Kyle demanded shrilly.

Dimitri laughed. "I figured you might be lying about the double cross the way you lied about the car in the driveway. We saw you let the girl inside. It's that friend of yours, isn't it? The one who's dating the cop. Where is she hiding?"

"She's not hiding anywhere. I don't know what you're talking about."

Mallory heard the sickening sound of a blow. "Quit lying. Where is she?" More blows. A moan.

"Stop. You're right. She's here. She threatened to turn me in, so I locked her in the powder room under the stairs. There's no way out."

"Give me the key."

"Why? She's no threat to us."

"Give me the key or I'll have Arlo break the door down."

Mallory looked around in vain for a weapon, but all she found were an abalone shell filled with guest soaps and a double roll of toilet paper, neither of which exactly qualified as lethal.

Fingers to the eyes. Knee to the groin. Then run like hell.
The instructional mantra of her first self-defense teacher
rang in her ears, good advice, though pretty tough talk
coming from someone named Sister Mary Joseph. Mallory balanced on the balls of her feet, ready to strike.

The key turned smoothly in the lock, the door
opened, and she froze, shocked into immobility for a
second. This was the first time she'd been up close and
personal with Arlo, and until now she hadn't realized
quite how big he was. Forget fingers to the eyes. She
couldn't reach his eyes even if she stood on tiptoe.

Okay, then. Knee to the groin it was. She connected
with a satisfying jolt that felled Arlo like a giant sequoia.

Then run like hell, she remembered. She hopped
nimbly over his prostrate form only to come face-to-face
with the business end of a .44 Magnum.

"Don't shoot her!" Kyle yelled. Mallory wondered if
her own eyes were bugged out as far as his.

Dimitri was yelling, too, calling her every name in
the book. Luckily for her self-esteem, the book was in
Russian and she didn't understand a word.

She kept waiting for her life to pass before her eyes,
but all she could think of was Brody's face when he'd
said, *Want to try it again?* and how she didn't want to die
because she was a survivor, dammit, not a victim, and she
really, really, really did want to try it again.

Fury distorted Dimitri's face; he sprayed little flecks
of spittle with each unintelligible word.

Kyle grabbed his arm. "Don't do anything you'll regret."

The Russian backhanded him with the pistol, and
Mallory screamed.

Kyle fell back against the wall, blood welling up from

a ragged tear in the skin near his left cheekbone. He put his hand to the cut, but the blood seeped through his fingers and ran down the back of his hand to stain his cuff crimson.

Dimitri leveled the gun at her once more. "Shut up, woman, or I'll shoot you where you stand."

Shocked to realize she was still screaming in a shrill, eerie voice she didn't recognize, Mallory clapped both hands over her mouth, reducing the noise to harsh, choking sobs.

Behind her, Arlo stirred. "Don't you kill her," he said. "This bitch is mine." He grabbed her in a bear hug that lifted her completely off her feet, shook her like a rag doll, then tossed her in the corner. Her teeth clattered together and she bit her tongue.

"You don't want to mess with her, Arlo," Kyle warned. He'd managed to stanch the bleeding with his handkerchief. "She's Detective Hunter's girlfriend. Believe me, you hurt her and you're going to have to answer to him."

"Hunter's woman, huh?" Arlo's slack-jawed grin scared her more than Dimitri's wild-eyed frenzy had. "I ain't scared of no cop, 'specially not that one. Maybe when I finish with her, I'll toss her in a Dumpster for him to find." His high-pitched giggle made her blood run cold.

"This is getting completely out of hand, guys." Kyle edged toward the stairs. "Let me get the money. You two can have it all. Split my share between you. Just take it and leave."

"Stay where you are!" Dimitri ordered. "Arlo will get the cash. Tell him where it is."

Kyle eyed his partners in crime, as if gauging how far

he could push them. Not far, to judge by Arlo's mulish expression and Dimitri's itchy trigger finger. A muscle twitched near Kyle's eye. He looked like a little kid trying to wink. Or a bigger kid trying not to cry. "Pull the bed away from the wall," he said. "The money's stashed in a little drawer hidden behind a fake wall socket."

With a grunt of satisfaction, the big man lumbered up the steps. Kyle shot her a defeated look.

Dammit, she thought, he couldn't give up. She caught his eye and mouthed the words, "It ain't over till it's over." But all he did was shake his head and stare glumly at the toes of his wing tips.

She glared at the Russian, but he wasn't paying any attention to her, either. Which should have offered a perfect opportunity to launch a counteroffensive. Unfortunately, Arlo's "hug" seemed to have temporarily severed communications between her brain and her body. The brain screamed "Get up!" but the body remained curled in the fetal position.

Dimitri glanced down at his Rolex, then up the stairs for the tenth time in two minutes. "What's taking him so long?"

"Probably decided he'd rather not share," she wheezed. It was hard to breathe, harder yet to talk. Arlo's imitation of a python had apparently bruised a couple ribs. "Bet he climbed out a window and down the trellis."

"Or slipped down the back stairs and out through the kitchen," Kyle suggested.

Now, that was more like it. She grinned at him.

"Shut up, both of you!" Dimitri shouted.

A sudden pounding on the front door riveted their attention. "Police, Mr. Brewster! Open up!"

Dimitri swore.

"Open up, Brewster, or we're taking the door down!"

Kyle took a step toward the door, but Dimitri waved him back with the gun.

"Open up! This is your last warning!"

"I've got a hostage!" Dimitri screamed. "Anyone steps through that door, I shoot her!"

Mallory didn't know whether they didn't believe him or just didn't hear him over the noise of the downpour, but in the next few seconds all hell broke loose.

Time seemed to slow to a crawl as half a dozen officers burst through the door in what looked like slow motion.

Screaming invectives—in English this time—Dimitri leveled the gun at her. At this distance he could hardly miss.

I'm dead, she thought. In the confusion, she focused on Brody's face, trying desperately to put all that she felt for him into her eyes.

"No!" Brody's scream echoed in her ears.

Kyle grabbed for Dimitri's gun arm. Dimitri jerked away, and the gun went off with an ear-shattering explosion. Kyle dropped to the floor as two burly cops wrestled the gun away from Dimitri.

Kyle's face was only inches from hers, but all she could see was the bright red stain spreading across the front of his white dress shirt like a big Georgia O'Keeffe poppy. "Hey, kiddo," he whispered. "It ain't over till it's over. Right?"

"Right," she said, but he didn't hear her.

❖————————❖

"I don't want to go home." Mallory had chosen a spot in the kitchen, deliberately distancing herself from the hubbub of the crime-scene investigation. She huddled in the blanket one of the paramedics had wrapped around her and frowned up at Brody. "Not alone. I'll wait for you."

He squatted down on his haunches so they were eye to eye. His were bloodshot, she noticed. And he needed a shave. But he was solid and real and alive, and she didn't want to go home without him. He took her hands in his. "Honey, I know what a shock all this has been. You need to go home, get out of those wet clothes and into a hot shower."

"No," she said, but before she could reinforce her refusal with logic, Regan Armstrong stuck her head in the door.

"Detective Hunter? Do you have a minute?"

Releasing Mallory's hands, Brody stood up. "What is it?"

"I'm the leak," she blurted. "A reporter from the *Gazette* made a snide remark about incompetent cops and I lost it, spilled my guts about Dairy-Best without considering the consequences. I'm sorry. I could have jeopardized the case." She looked sick.

"Noted," Brody said.

Another officer shoved past her, and she left without another word.

"What do you want, Hawkins?" Brody asked impatiently.

"You know that APB we put out? Paiute County deputy just reported sighting a Ford van, possibly our suspect, heading west on US 20."

Arlo, she thought. He'd slipped out the back in all the confusion.

"Also, the guy from the funeral home wants to know who to contact as next of kin."

Dolph? she wondered. Or maybe not. He'd been the anonymous informant.

"I'll talk to him in a minute," Brody said. The officer left and Brody turned back to her with an expression that brooked no argument. "You've had enough. I'll get someone to drive you home."

"But—"

"God knows how long it's going to take to finish up here, but as soon as I'm done, I'll stop by. I promise."

"I'll be waiting," she said, which reminded her of all the times she'd waited for him in the last two weeks—with Kyle keeping her company on more than one occasion—and she started to cry in big, racking sobs.

"Don't," said Brody. He gathered her into his arms, wet clothes, blanket, tears, and all, holding her close, patting her back, whispering comforting nonsense. And she wasn't sure, but she thought maybe he even cried a little himself.

"Why did he do it?" she asked when she could talk again.

"Because he loved you." Brody kissed her forehead. "Because he knew I loved you too."

Cesar Rios drove her back to her house, a second officer following in a patrol car. He parked in her usual spot, then walked her to the door like a polite date. "Brody said to make sure you lock the door."

She summoned up a wisp of a smile. "Thanks. I will.

And tell Brody something for me, okay? Tell him I'll be waiting."

Cesar gave her two thumbs up, then jogged out to the patrol car parked at the curb. She waved them off, then went inside and locked the door.

The warmth of the shower felt so good, she lingered under the spray for three-quarters of an hour and would have stayed even longer if the hot water hadn't given out. Wrapping herself in a towel, she wandered back to her bedroom. She stopped dead in the doorway, shock immobilizing her.

A huge man, dressed in fatigues, army boots, and a camouflage tank top that bared his hairy back, was pawing through her lingerie drawer. He spun around to face her, and she saw it was Arlo. Her red satin chemise dangled from the tip of his hunting knife by one narrow strap. "Real neighborly of you to leave the key under the flowerpot, girlie." He tossed her the chemise. "Put it on."

It landed at her feet like a pool of blood.

"When I saw the bag of lingerie in your truck," she said, "I thought you were a cross-dresser, but all those frilly pieces of underwear were trophies, weren't they?"

"I spread 'em on my pillow at night so's I can smell the fear and remember." A slack-jawed grin split his face. "Put it on," he said again.

Rage shuddered through her. "If you're going to rape me, then do it, but don't expect me to play along with your sick fantasies."

His eyes widened, showing white all around the irises, and he charged with a roar. She threw the towel in his face, whirled, and bolted for the bathroom, slamming and locking the door after her, though she knew it offered only an illusion of safety. Not even solid oak could stop that human battering ram.

"Open the damn door, bitch!"

Hoping to trick him, she slid the window open, then slipped behind the bi-fold doors that hid her washer and dryer.

"I'm gonna slice you up for this. I'm gonna make you pay."

As he started telling her exactly how he was going to make her pay, Mallory shut her ears to his obscenities, concentrating fiercely on the task at hand. Standing on the washing machine, she lifted the trapdoor that gave access to the attic, then hoisted herself through just as the bathroom door gave in a splintering crash. Ignoring his howl of thwarted rage, she quietly lowered the trapdoor and groped her way along the rafters toward the second access door in the garage. And escape.

In response to a report of a green minivan blocking an alley half a block away, three police cars and Brody's Jeep pulled to the curb in front of Mallory's. Brody heard the bellowing before he was halfway to the front door and knew with a sick certainty that they'd found their missing suspect. He motioned the others to surround the house while he banged on the front door. "Mallory? Can you hear me? Are you in there?"

"Detective, this way!" Officer Armstrong beckoned from the corner of the house with a wave of her flashlight. "We got him."

Brody followed her around back, moving as quickly as he could. The rain had slacked off to a drizzle, but the ground underfoot was spongy and slick.

As he came around the corner he saw Arlo Davis, Jr., a.k.a., GI Joe, hanging out of Mallory's narrow bathroom window, his hips and belly wedged fast, his arms thrashing wildly like the antennae of some giant prehistoric insect.

"Cuff him," he said. "Club him if you have to."

While officers were immobilizing Davis's wrists Brody grabbed a tuft of his hair and jerked his head up. "Where's Mallory?"

"How the hell should I know? When I get ahold of that bitch, though, she's gonna—"

Brody ignored the rest of the tirade. He'd heard enough to know that she'd eluded her would-be rapist. Mallory was safe. That was what mattered.

"Detective?" Hawkins tapped him on the shoulder.

"Did you find her?"

"In the garage." The two set off at a trot.

"Is she all right?"

"We think so, sir. Can't tell for sure. She won't come down."

"Down? I thought you said she was in the garage."

"She is, sir. In the attic, but she says she won't come down for anyone but you."

My God, he thought as he followed Hawkins into the garage, she must be scared to death. "Mallory? Honey, it's Brody. Come on down. You're safe. We caught the scumbag."

"Brody, make everyone else leave, okay? Then I want you to close the garage door."

"But why?"

"Don't argue, please. Just do it." Her voice held a note of desperation.

He shooed the others out and rolled the big door

down. "Okay," he said. "I did as you asked. Mind telling me what this is all about?"

"Stand under the trapdoor. There isn't a ladder. You're going to have to catch me."

She lowered herself from the hole in the ceiling, then dropped neatly into his arms, naked and shivering.

Her eyes were wide and glassy as marbles, her skin as pale and cold as marble. "I didn't let him make me a victim," she said.

"No, you were very brave, very resourceful." He set her down as carefully as if she were made of glass, stripped off his jacket, and wrapped it around her.

"She'll be all right. Just keep her warm," Mallory had heard the doctor tell Brody. So he'd added a couple of blankets to her bed and tucked a hot-water bottle down by her feet when all she really wanted was his big, warm body wrapped around hers.

Then her mother'd shown up and darned near chicken-souped her to death; she'd finally dozed off in self-defense. She woke up a little after ten, feeling pretty good until she realized it was Monday and she was supposed to be in math class introducing her fifth graders to the mysteries of the multiplicative inverse.

"Don't fret," April said. "I called your principal. She's hired a sub to cover for the next few days." Her mother pulled the quilt straight and tucked it under Mallory's chin. "I have a few errands to run, but Brody's asleep in the next room. Just yell if you need anything."

Mallory waited until she heard her mother drive away, then slipped out of bed and into Brody's room. He looked ten years younger with his face relaxed, the thick, dark lashes fanned out against his cheeks. "Brody?" she whispered.

His eyelashes fluttered open. When he saw who it was, he struggled to a sitting position, stifling a yawn. "You shouldn't be out of bed."

"You're absolutely right," she said, and climbed in next to him, cuddling up to his side.

"What are you doing, Mallory?"

"Don't worry. My mother gave me permission." She pressed herself closer, trailing her fingertips across the ridged muscle of his exposed chest.

He gave an involuntary shudder. "For this?"

Mallory nibbled at his earlobe. "She said to see you if I needed anything. And Brody"—she walked her fingers down the center of his abdomen—"what I need is you. I love you desperately. And I don't care if you're the commitment type or not. You're my type, and that's all that matters."

"No, it's not." He grabbed her wandering hand and pressed it to his chest, where his heart thumped an agitated rhythm. "Feel that, honey? That's what happens every time I think of you." He took a deep breath. "Last night when I saw that gun pointed at your head, I damned near had a heart attack."

Mallory's throat grew tight.

"I love you, Mallory, but sex is only a small part of it. I want to live with you, have children with you, grow old with you." He swallowed hard. "Marry me?"

"Oh, yes," she said, and kissed him.

Depths, he thought. *Soft, warm, loving depths.*

THE EDITORS' CORNER

Shake off those stuffy winter doldrums and get ready for the first scents of spring, which are sure to charm you into going outside. But don't forget to pack the new April LOVESWEPTs in your picnic basket. We have some of your favorite authors delivering terrifically unique, terrifically LOVESWEPT stories that are guaranteed to make springtime bloom in your heart. Enjoy!

Logan Blackstone plays **DARK KNIGHT** to Scottie Giardi's secret agent in Donna Kauffman's steamy new LOVESWEPT, #882. Scottie has a mission to accomplish—to keep Logan busy so that he can't interfere with a covert plan that's been in motion for months. But Logan has plans of his own. He's on the hunt for his long-lost twin brother, Lucas, who's involved in a cult. Stuck together in a cabin, the two form a tenuous relationship of passion and respect, not to mention constant bickering and bantering. Logan and Scottie are two kindred souls who are running from themselves, but will they acknowledge that it's time to stop fearing yesterday and look forward to tomorrow? Donna Kauffman answers that question in this achingly intense story of perfectly matched adversaries.

In Kathy Lynn Emerson's new LOVESWEPT, #883, Chase Forster and Leslie Baynton promise to be together **SIGHT UNSEEN.** Convinced by her sister that she's become the stereotypical old-maid librarian, complete with feline companion, Leslie knows it's time for a change in her life. So when Chase sends an E-mail asking, "Will you be my E-mail-order bride?" Leslie answers with a very uncharacteristic yes. Granted, getting married to a man she's met only by computer is a little crazy, but as soon as she hears Chase's warm voice, she knows she's made the right decision. Chase has to raise his brother's children and he thinks Leslie would make a terrific role model for the troubled teens. So a makeshift family is born. With more than a few surprises up her sleeve, Kathy explores the intricacies of a thoroughly modern marriage.

Well-received author Kristen Robinette brings us **FLIRTING WITH FIRE,** LOVESWEPT #884. Danger had Samantha Delaney on the run, and after coming to live in the small southern town of Scottsdale, Georgia, she thought for sure that she had escaped its clutches. Samantha answers Daniel Caldwell's ad for an apartment for rent and moves into the east wing of his antebellum home. Daniel, with a secret of his own locked away in the caretaker's cottage, wonders at the demons haunting his lovely tenant's eyes. Suddenly the threats are back and Samantha no longer knows who she can turn to—her devastatingly handsome landlord or her faithful and loyal assistant. Kristen Robinette weaves an intricate and suspenseful tale that is as emotionally compelling as it is exquisitely romantic.

In Jill Shalvis's **THE HARDER THEY FALL**, LOVESWEPT #885, Trisha Mallory falls out of the ceiling into Dr. Hunter Adams's arms, and thus begins a stormy relationship that makes for great laughs and huge catastrophes. Whether she's forgetting to close refrigerator doors or rearranging his car's fender, Trisha seems to wreak havoc wherever she goes. And for Hunter, a stuffy space scientist (Trisha's words, not ours), having Trisha as a neighbor is going to be the end of him. After living with incredibly flighty parents, Hunter has vowed that never again will his life be unorganized, while Trisha has vowed that the effects of her strict upbringing will not cloud her zest for life. Jill Shalvis's fast-paced romp pairs two mismatched lovers who are stunned to discover they're mad for each other.

Happy reading!

With warmest wishes,

Susann Brailey

Joy Abella

Susann Brailey   Joy Abella
Senior Editor   Administrative Editor

P.S. Look for these women's fiction titles coming in April! Dubbed by *USA Today* as "one of the hottest and most prolific romance writers today," *New York Times* bestseller Amanda Quick delivers **WITH THIS RING,** in which a villain lurks in the netherworld of London, waiting for authoress Beatrice Poole and the Earl of Monkcrest to unearth the Forbidden Rings—knowing that when they do, that day will be their last. Now available in paperback is *New York Times* bestseller Tami Hoag's **A THIN DARK LINE,** a breathtakingly sensual novel filled with heart-stopping suspense when the boundaries between the law and justice and love and murder are crossed. From nationally bestselling Teresa Medeiros comes a new romance blockbuster, **NOBODY'S DARLING.** When young Bostonian Esmerelda Fine hires her brother's accused murderer to help track her brother down, the adventure and passion have just begun. . . . Bantam newcomer Katie Rose presents **A HINT OF MISCHIEF.** Three beautiful sisters set Victorian New York society—and a sinfully attractive businessman—on its ear when they start performing séances, in this clever historical romance of nineteenth-century America. And immediately following this page, preview the Bantam women's fiction titles on sale in March!

For current information on Bantam's women's fiction, visit our Web site, *Isn't It Romantic*, at the following address: **http://www.bdd.com/romance**

Don't miss these extraordinary
novels from Bantam Books!

On Sale in March:

PUBLIC SECRETS
by Nora Roberts

BIRTHDAY GIRLS
by Jean Stone

SHOTGUN GROOM
by Sandra Chastain

"Move over, Sidney Sheldon: the world has a new master of romantic suspense, and her name is Nora Roberts."—Rex Reed

Emma, beautiful, intelligent, radiantly talented, she lives in a star-studded world of wealth and privilege. But she is about to discover that fame is no protection at all when someone wants you dead. . . .

PUBLIC SECRETS
by Nora Roberts

All she has to do is close her eyes and remember the day Brian McAvoy swept into her life. A frightened toddler, she didn't know then that she was his illegitimate daughter or that he was pop music's rising star. All she knew was that with Brian, his band mates, and his new wife, she felt safe. And when her baby brother arrived, Emma thought she was the luckiest girl in the world . . . until the night a botched kidnapping attempt shattered all their lives . . . and destroyed Emma's happiness.

Yet now, even though Emma is still haunted by flashes of memory from that fateful night, she has survived. She's carved out a thrilling career and even dared to fall rapturously in love. But the man who will become her husband isn't all that he seems. And Emma is about to awaken to the chilling knowledge that the darkest secret of all is the one buried in her mind—a secret that someone may kill to keep.

When Emma woke, the floor was vibrating with the bass from the stereo. She lay quietly a moment listening, trying as she did from time to time to recognize the song from the beat alone.

She'd gotten used to the parties. Her da liked to have people around. Lots of music, lots of laughing. When she was older, she would go to parties, too.

Bev always made sure the house was very clean before the guests arrived. That was silly, really, Emma thought. In the morning, the house was a terrible mess with smelly glasses and overflowing ashtrays. More often than not a few of the guests would be sprawled over the sofas and chairs amid the clutter.

Emma wondered what it would be like to sit up all night, talking, laughing, listening to music. When you were grown up, no one told you when you had to go to bed, or have a bath.

With a sigh, she rolled over on her back. The music was faster now. She could feel the driving bass pulse in the walls. And something else. Footsteps, coming down the hall, Emma thought. Miss Wallingsford. She prepared to close her eyes and feign sleep when another thought occurred to her. Perhaps it was Da or Mum passing through to check on her and Darren. If it was, she could pretend to have just woken, then she could persuade them to tell her about the party.

But the footsteps passed by. She sat up clutching Charlie. She'd wanted company, even if only for a moment or two. She wanted to talk about the party, or the trip to New York. She wanted to know what song was playing. She sat a moment, a small, sleepy child in a pink nightgown, bathed by the cheerful glow of a Mickey Mouse night-light.

She thought she heard Darren crying. Straightening, she strained to listen. She was certain she heard Darren's cranky tears over the pulse of the music. Automatically she climbed out of bed, tucking Charlie under one arm. She would sit with Darren until he quieted, and leave Charlie to watch over him through the rest of the night.

The hallway was dark, which surprised her. A light always burned there in case Emma had to use the bathroom during the night. She had a bad moment at the doorway, imagining the things that lurked in the shadowy corners. She wanted to stay in her room with the grinning Mickey.

Then Darren let out a yowling cry.

There was nothing in the corners, Emma told herself as she started down the dark hallway. There was nothing there at all. No monsters, no ghosts, no squishy or slithering things.

It was the Beatles playing now.

Emma wet her lips. Just the dark, just the dark, she told herself. Her eyes had adjusted to the dark by the time she'd reached Darren's door. It was closed. That was wrong, too. His door was always left open so he could be heard easily when awakened.

She reached out, then jumped as she thought she heard something move behind her. Heart pumping, she turned to scan the dark hallway. Shifting shadows towered into nameless monsters, making sweat break out on her brow and back.

Nothing there, nothing there, she told herself, and Darren was crying his lungs out.

She turned the knob and pushed the door open.

"Come together," Lennon sang. "Over me."

There were two men in the room. One was holding Darren, struggling to keep him still while the baby screamed in fear and anger. The other had something in his hand, something that the light from the giraffe lamp on the dresser caused to glint.

"What are you doing?"

The man whirled at her voice. He wasn't a doctor, Emma thought as she made out the needle in his hand. She recognized him, and knew he wasn't a doctor. And Darren wasn't sick.

The other man swore, a short spurt of ugly words, while he fought to keep Darren from wriggling out of his arms.

"Emma," the man she knew said in a calm, friendly voice. He smiled. It was a false smile, an angry smile. She noted it, and that he still held the needle as he stepped toward her. She turned and ran.

Behind her she heard Darren call out. *"Ma!"*

Sobbing, she raced down the hall. There were monsters, her panicked mind taunted. There were monsters and things with snappy teeth in the shadows. They were coming after her now.

He nearly caught the trailing edge of her nightgown. Swearing, he dove for her. His hand skimmed over her ankle, slid off. She yelped as though she'd been scalded. As she reached the top of the stairs, she screamed for her father, shrieking his name over and over again.

Then her legs tangled. She tumbled down the flight of stairs.

In the kitchen, someone sat on the counter and ordered fifty pizzas. Shaking her head, Bev checked the freezer for ice. No one used more ice than Americans. As an afterthought, she dropped a cube in her warming wine. When in Rome, she decided, then turned toward the door.

She met Brian on the threshold.

Grinning, he hooked an arm around her waist and gave her a long, lazy kiss. "Hi."

"Hi." Still holding the wine, she linked her hands behind his neck. "Bri."

"Hmm?"

"Who are all these people?"

He laughed, nuzzling into her neck. "You've got me." The scent of her had him hardening. Moving to the sinuous beat of the Lennon/McCartney number, he brought her against him. "What do you say we take a trip upstairs and leave them the rest of the house."

"That's rude." But she moved against him. "Wicked, rude, and the best idea I've heard in hours."

"Well, then . . ." He made a halfhearted attempt to pick her up, sent them both teetering. Wine spilled cool down his back as Bev giggled. "Maybe you can carry me," he said, then heard Emma scream.

He rammed into a small table as he turned. Dizzy from drugs and booze, he stumbled, righted himself, and rushed into the foyer. There were people already gathered. Pushing through them, he saw her crumpled at the foot of the steps.

"Emma. My God." He was terrified to touch her. There was blood at the corner of her mouth. With one trembling finger, he wiped it away. He looked up into a sea of faces, a blur of color, all unrecognizable. His stomach clenched, then tried to heave itself into his throat.

"Call an ambulance," he managed, then bent over her again.

"Don't move her." Bev's face was chalk-white as she knelt beside him. "I don't think you're supposed to move her. We need a blanket." Some quick-witted soul was already thrusting a daisy afghan into her hands. "She'll be all right, Bri." Carefully, Bev smoothed the blanket over her. "She'll be just fine."

He closed his eyes, shook his head to clear it. But when he opened them again, Emma was still lying, dead-white, on the floor. There was too much noise. The music echoing off the ceilings, the voices murmuring, muttering all around. He felt a hand on his shoulder. A quick, reassuring squeeze.

"Ambulance is on the way," P.M. told him. "Hold on, Bri."

"Get them out," he whispered. He looked up and into Johnno's shocked, pale face. "Get them out of here."

With a nod, Johnno began to urge people along. The door was open, the night bright with floodlights and headlights when they heard the wail of the sirens.

"I'm going to go up," Bev said calmly. "Tell Alice what's happened, check on Darren. We'll go to the hospital with her. She's going to be fine, Brian. I know it."

He could only nod and stare down at Emma's still, pale face. He couldn't leave her. If he had dared, he would have gone into the bathroom, stuck a finger down his throat, and tried to rid his body of some of the chemicals he'd pumped into it that night.

It was all like a dream, he thought, a floaty, unhappy dream. Until he looked at Emma's face. Then it was real, much too real.

The *Abbey Road* album was still playing, the sly cut about murder. Maxwell's silver hammer was coming down.

"Bri." Johnno put a hand on his arm. "Move back now, so they can tend to her."

"What?"

"Move back." Gently Johnno eased him to his feet. "They need to have a look at her."

Dazed, Brian watched the ambulance attendants move in and crouch over his daughter. "She must have fallen all the way down the stairs."

"She'll be all right." Johnno sent a helpless look toward P.M. as they flanked Brian. "Little girls are tougher than they look."

"That's right." A bit unsteady on his feet, Stevie stood behind Brian with both hands on his shoulders. "Our Emma won't let a tumble down the stairs hold her up for long."

"We'll go to the hospital with you." Pete moved over to join them. Together they watched as Emma was carefully lifted onto a stretcher.

Upstairs, Bev screamed . . . and screamed and screamed, until the sound filled every corner of the house.

A gifted storyteller who truly "understands the human heart,"* Jean Stone returns with another deeply enthralling tale, this one about three women facing fifty—and determined to change their lives. . . .

BIRTHDAY GIRLS

by Jean Stone

Once they were childhood friends who celebrated birthdays together, sharing laughter and tears and heartfelt dreams. Then they lost touch. Yet now, on the brink of turning fifty, one of them is desperate enough to contact the others—looking for more than an innocent reunion. . . .

Abigail is a star, a new Martha Stewart whose weekly TV show has won her millions of fans. Maddie is a brilliant photographer under contract with a hip magazine. And daredevil Kris is a writer whose taut thrillers have been on bestseller lists for years. But one of them carries a dark, tormenting secret; another is obsessed with the man she loved and lost; a third would give anything to start over; and all are haunted by the stark passage of time.

So what will the friends do? They'll share their birthday wishes just like before, only this time they'll go to any lengths to make sure their wishes come true. . . .

* The Literary Times

"It would be nice if one of you said something."

Maddie realized she was staring at Abigail—the woman who had everything any woman in the world could possibly ever want, except, of course, kids; but then again, Kris hadn't wanted any either but now she did and, oh God, this was all so confusing it made her head hurt. She blinked. "Maybe you should clarify."

Kris laughed. "I think our queen of the kitchen is saying she wants out."

"*Out*," Abigail said. "Yes, that's a good word. All my life I've been trying to please others. First it was Grandfather. Then Edmund. Now the entire freaking world."

Maddie watched as Abigail walked over to the fireplace, ran her finger across the carved marble mantel, then looked up to the portraits of her grandfather and his father before him. It struck her that this was not the same, unretouched woman who posed on the cover of *In the Rose Garden with Abigail;* this was not the same woman who had always been in control. She was pale and drawn; she was . . . vulnerable. God, in all the years Maddie had known her, she'd never once thought of Abigail Hardy as vulnerable.

"I don't even have a clue who I am," Abigail said softly. "By the time I am fifty I need to find out. But I'm not going to learn it by pretending to be someone I no longer want to be."

Maddie now realized that Abigail must definitely have hit menopause. It was the only answer that made any sense. She tried to sound compassionate as she asked, "Have you seen a gynecologist?"

Abigail whipped around. "Don't blame my hormones, Maddie. I've hated every minute of my life for years. Most of all, I hate the damn 'empire' I worked so hard to create. Now I'm going to do something about it."

It was difficult to believe that Abigail was serious. She had done so much with her life, had touched so many people. How would millions of women react without Abigail Hardy in their kitchens each week? How would Sophie react? Maddie wanted to ask if there would be reruns, but somehow that didn't seem appropriate. Still, the thought of no longer having to endure the dinner-of-the-week was not unappealing.

Kris stood and moved over to Abigail. "I say go for it, girl. What the hell, we only live once."

"Thanks, Kris. I knew I could count on you."

Maddie wondered what Betty Ann would have said, in her cherub-like, childlike way. "Maybe you should take it a step at a time," she replied, trying to sound encouraging. "Start with a separation from Edmund. Cut down on your work schedule. Travel. Something less . . . drastic." Her words sounded thin. She traced the curves of the paisley brocade on the sofa.

"I don't think you get it, Maddie. This isn't like a diet. I'm not trying to wean myself off chocolate. If I'm going to do this, I've got to do it. Sever the ties. All of them."

"Including divorce?" Maddie asked.

"Sorry, Maddie," Kris said. "Sometimes that's what it takes to move on."

But Abigail was shaking her head. "No. I'm not going to get a divorce."

"What then?" Maddie asked.

"I'm going to disappear. And you are going to help me fake my death."

Kris whistled. "Holy shit, you're serious."

Abigail raised her chin. "Very."

"You can't do that," Maddie protested. "You can't just drop off the face of the earth and make people think you're . . . dead."

"It's the only way. My life is too complicated. Untangling the business alone would be a nightmare. And it could take years."

It hadn't taken years for Parker to "untangle" Maddie from *Our World.* A few swipes of the pen on the dotted line and—presto—she was out. Of course, the magazine had still been in its infancy. Of course, there had been no profits to make it look valuable. Of course, Maddie had been stupid.

"You two are the only ones I can trust," Abigail continued. "No one but the three of us can know the truth. Maddie gets her ex-husband, Kris gets her baby, and I get . . . out. It's all or nothing. Do we have a deal?"

Maddie chanced a glance at Kris. Kris grinned back at her. So Abigail *had* had an agenda. Now they knew. "When do you plan to do this?"

"Not until your wishes have come true. Unless, of course, either of you changes her mind. I, for one, won't."

The irony did not escape Maddie. Here she was, trying to get her life back, and here Abigail was, trying to throw hers away. As for Kris, well, who knew about Kris. Next week she'd probably be off in Bora Bora and forget the whole thing.

"So," Kris asked, "where do we start?"

"Maddie made her wish first, so let's begin with her."

"That should be easy," Kris said. "Men are my specialty."

Folding her hands in her lap, Maddie wondered which one of them was the craziest.

From
Sandra Chastain,
bestselling author of
Raven and the Cowboy, comes

SHOTGUN GROOM

A Tennessee belle with her sights aimed at a rugged Texan's heart, Lily Towns was determined to marry Matt Logan, even if she had to use her shotgun to get him to the altar. But confirmed bachelor Matt Logan wasn't looking for a bride, especially one sexy, sensual Memphis belle.

When the only woman on the coach stepped down onto the plank sidewalk at the stage office, Matt knew immediately that it was too late to whisk her away. This was one time his private business was likely to become public. Drawing Racer to a stop behind a stack of wooden kegs, he sat helplessly watching the woman smile at everyone in sight.

"Welcome to Blue Station," Luther said, his head bobbing like a chicken picking up corn.

"Yes, ma'am," Ambrose Wells, the town's self-appointed mayor, said, suddenly appearing on the platform as if meeting the stage were part of the banker's everyday duties. "I'm the president of the Blue Station Banking Company, Miss . . ."

"Townsend, Miss Lillian Townsend. I'm so very pleased to meet . . . all of you."

Lillian Townsend? Even the name was much

too elegant for the Double L. Lillian Townsend ought to be one of those entertainers who traveled around making stage appearances, instead of this elegant vision of sunlight and satin who'd come here to be a Texas bride.

"And what brings you to Blue Station, Miss Townsend?" Wells asked, still holding her hand as if he didn't trust the good fortune that brought such a beauty to town. "Is someone meeting you?"

"Oh yes, I'm being met by my future husband."

The expression on the banker's face froze and he looked at Luther in disbelief. Matt swore silently from his vantage point.

Apparently Luther hadn't shared the information that Matt Logan was getting married, though he had obviously told Wells a new woman was coming on the stage. But Lillian Townsend was about to spread the news.

"Future husband?" Wells questioned, not bothering to conceal his surprise.

"Why, yes. Matt Logan. He and his brother, Jim, have a cattle ranch nearby, I believe."

Christ! Now she'd done it. Matt had always been a very private man, keeping himself away from involvement with the townspeople. He'd claimed that there were no women in Blue Springs, but that hadn't been entirely true. There were women, too many women, and their constant matchmaking made his life miserable.

Now this woman was announcing to the world that she'd come to marry one of the Logan brothers. Matt had to stop her quick.

On Sale in April:

WITH THIS RING
by *Amanda Quick*

A THIN DARK LINE
by *Tami Hoag*

NOBODY'S DARLING
by *Teresa Medeiros*

A HINT OF MISCHIEF
by *Katie Rose*

Bestselling Historical Women's Fiction

⚜ AMANDA QUICK ⚜

____28354-5 SEDUCTION ...$6.50/$8.99 Canada

____28932-2 SCANDAL ....$6.50/$8.99

____28594-7 SURRENDER ....$6.50/$8.99

____29325-7 RENDEZVOUS ....$6.50/$8.99

____29315-X RECKLESS ....$6.50/$8.99

____29316-8 RAVISHED ....$6.50/$8.99

____29317-6 DANGEROUS ....$6.50/$8.99

____56506-0 DECEPTION ....$6.50/$8.99

____56153-7 DESIRE ....$6.50/$8.99

____56940-6 MISTRESS ....$6.50/$8.99

____57159-1 MYSTIQUE ....$6.50/$7.99

____57190-7 MISCHIEF ....$6.50/$8.99

____57407-8 AFFAIR ....$6.99/$8.99

⚜ IRIS JOHANSEN ⚜

____29871-2 LAST BRIDGE HOME ...$5.50/$7.50

____29604-3 THE GOLDEN
                    BARBARIAN ....$6.99/$8.99

____29244-7 REAP THE WIND ......$5.99/$7.50

____29032-0 STORM WINDS ....$6.99/$8.99

Ask for these books at your local bookstore or use this page to order.

Please send me the books I have checked above. I am enclosing $____ (add $2.50 to cover postage and handling). Send check or money order, no cash or C.O.D.'s, please.

Name _____

Address _____

City/State/Zip _____

Send order to: Bantam Books, Dept. FN 16, 2451 S. Wolf Rd., Des Plaines, IL 60018
Allow four to six weeks for delivery.
Prices and availability subject to change without notice.   FN 16 3/98

Bestselling Historical Women's Fiction

❧ IRIS JOHANSEN ❧

____ 28855-5 THE WIND DANCER ...$5.99/$6.99

____ 29968-9 THE TIGER PRINCE ...$6.99/$8.99

____ 29944-1 THE MAGNIFICENT

ROGUE ....$6.99/$8.99

____ 29945-X BELOVED SCOUNDREL .$6.99/$8.99

____ 29946-8 MIDNIGHT WARRIOR ..$6.99/$8.99

____ 29947-6 DARK RIDER ....$6.99/$8.99

____ 56990-2 LION'S BRIDE ....$6.99/$8.99

____ 56991-0 THE UGLY DUCKLING...$5.99/$7.99

____ 57181-8 LONG AFTER MIDNIGHT.$6.99/$8.99

____ 10616-3 AND THEN YOU DIE....$22.95/$29.95

❧ TERESA MEDEIROS ❧

____ 29407-5 HEATHER AND VELVET .$5.99/$7.50

____ 29409-1 ONCE AN ANGEL .....$5.99/$7.99

____ 29408-3 A WHISPER OF ROSES .$5.99/$7.99

____ 56332-7 THIEF OF HEARTS .....$5.50/$6.99

____ 56333-5 FAIREST OF THEM ALL .$5.99/$7.50

____ 56334-3 BREATH OF MAGIC ....$5.99/$7.99

____ 57623-2 SHADOWS AND LACE ...$5.99/$7.99

____ 57500-7 TOUCH OF

ENCHANTMENT.........$5.99/$7.99

Ask for these books at your local bookstore or use this page to order.

Please send me the books I have checked above. I am enclosing $____ (add $2.50 to cover postage and handling). Send check or money order, no cash or C.O.D.'s, please.

Name _____

Address _____

City/State/Zip _____

Send order to: Bantam Books, Dept. FN 16, 2451 S. Wolf Rd., Des Plaines, IL 60018
Allow four to six weeks for delivery.
Prices and availability subject to change without notice.   FN 16 3/98